Praise for *Buyer Beware* by John Lutz

"Lutz seldom leaves you at a loss for page-turning questions."   —*Publishers Weekly*

"In the course of its telling, this novel yields many pleasures. A fine book."
—*1001 Midnights*

"Lutz brings enormous talent to every book and especially so in *Buyer Beware*."
—*Mystery Scene*

"One of the best and most unusual novels in the history of private eye fiction."
—*Cedar Rapids Gazette*

Buyer Beware

JOHN LUTZ

Carroll & Graf Publishers, Inc.
New York

Carroll & Graf Publishers, Inc.
260 Fifth Avenue
New York, NY 10001

ISBN: 0-88184-840-9

Manufactured in the United States of America

For Malzberg and Pronzini,
selfless sorts who pointed the way

Caveat emptor quia ignorare non debuit quod jus alienum emit.

Let the buyer beware because he should not be ignorant of the property that he is buying.

Buyer Beware

1

Summer was struggling hard at birth. Hail in artillerylike salvos battered the metal roof and sides of my forty-foot house trailer, as it had, interspersed with heavy rain, for the past two hours.

As time passes, hail striking the surface of a house trailer seems to take on more of a metallic ring. I was becoming slightly shell-shocked and vowed again to myself to move into an apartment as soon as possible.

But even as I made my vow I knew I wouldn't move. Not many apartment managers let you run a business out of your place of residence, and I had written permission from Mel Hardin, owner of Trailer Haven, to combine home and office here. Not a prestigious address, maybe, but prestige doesn't cook into much of a meal.

The pace of the hail picked up, and I rose from the sofa, went into the dollhouse bathroom and washed down two aspirin with a glass of tepid water. On my return from the bathroom I noticed an indistinct damp spot on the gold shag carpet where it met the south wall of the trailer. The damned thing leaked! I would tell Hardin about that tomorrow.

Before sitting down again on the sofa, I reached out and turned up the volume on the portable TV so I could better understand the six o'clock news, that and sometimes the ten o'clock report being the only programs I watched on television besides an occasional

11

sporting event. A wholesomely attractive girl was teasing viewers with the weather forecast just then, demonstrating with a pointer how a warm front moving in from the Southeast was causing all kinds of trouble. She seemed happy about it.

Her explanation did account for the hail, but not for the determined rasping of my door buzzer. I rose again from the sofa, almost afraid to let in somebody who was crazy enough to be outside in this kind of weather. Through the south window I saw horizontal fingers of lightning rend the sky over perfectly aligned trailer roofs and TV antennas, like something out of an updated Frankenstein movie.

The man standing beneath the metal awning that sheltered my trailer door fit right into the movie. He was moderately tall, hatless, dark-haired and full-bearded. His long black raincoat matched the black umbrella he held angled into the wind.

"Hey," he said, spoiling the theatrical effect, "you Mr. Nudger?"

I nodded, stepping back to let him inside, noticing the four- or five-year-old compact sedan he must have got out of parked near the rack of mailboxes that served this side of the graveled street.

He was about six feet tall, a shade over my height, and now that he was inside and his face wasn't contorted to the violent weather, I saw that he had even, pleasant features and straight-ahead brown eyes. His umbrella was still in good shape after protecting him from the hail, and he folded it carefully and leaned it against the wall by the door.

As I motioned him farther inside so he could sit down, I speculated on whether he was an insurance salesman, evangelist or client. He carried no briefcase, and he hadn't yet smiled. Could be a client. Maybe he was desperate, after trying all the other confidential investigators in the directory. Not much to choose from

12

there. It's a precarious way to make a living. You need a specialty.

"I'm Gordon Clark," he said, "and I'm here on business."

Good. I liked the ones who got to the point. I took his wet raincoat and draped it over the wooden back of a chair. Beneath his coat he was wearing dark slacks and a light-tan leisure jacket, and there was a tight muscularity about the forward set of his shoulders. He sat down as if he'd been standing too long. He was troubled.

"You are Mr. Nudger, of Nudger Investigations, aren't you?"

"The same, Mr. Clark. Alo Nudger." I bent to shake hands with him and continued standing, slipping my hands into my pockets.

"Alo?"

"Short for Aloysious, long for Al, as I used to tell the ladies."

"Sure. I want to hire you."

"You must want to hire me badly to come out in this kind of weather."

"I don't let the weather interfere with what I have to do, Mr. Nudger."

I looked at him more closely. I had gauged him wrong. He was in his late twenties, and his dark beard, no longer matted with rivulets of rainwater, was precisely trimmed in the manner of a stylish up-and-comer rather than in the natural, free-swinging style of youth. His jacket was slightly worn, but it appeared expensively tailored, though possibly for someone else.

"Did you choose my name from the telephone directory?"

He shook his head. "You were recommended by an acquaintance who was once involved in one of your cases—a Mrs. Gloria Fallering."

I sat on the sofa opposite Clark's chair. "I remember

13

her—a four-year-old son. She should hate my guts."

"She does. That's what recommended you to me."

I had to laugh. The hail had stopped suddenly, and the TV I'd forgotten was on was blaring an important message about irregularity. I reached over and switched it off.

"You used to be Mr. Happy on television, didn't you?" Clark said.

"That was me," I admitted. "The clown cop who introduced safety cartoons for the kiddies."

"It must have paid good, being Mr. Happy."

"But it wasn't police work. I like kids, but three years of Mr. Happy was enough." The real reason I was no longer Mr. Happy was none of his concern.

"So that's how you got into kidnapping."

"More or less. Is that why you want to hire me?"

"Yes." Clark crossed his arms and leaned back, setting himself to do some talking. "My wife, Joan, and I were married eight years ago. . . ."

"Begin at the end," I told him.

Clark smiled for the first time, though not a smile to light up the room. "A little over a year ago we got our divorce. Irreconcilable differences. They say some couples can be better friends, if not lovers, after a divorce. That wasn't true in our case. Looking back on it, though, I guess Melissa was the one thing we really fought about."

"Melissa?"

"Our seven-year-old daughter. At first Joan didn't seem to resent me using my visitation rights to see her, but about six months ago her attitude changed. I think there was another man."

"From before or after the divorce?"

"After, I'm sure," Clark said without hesitation.

"Do you know where your ex-wife and the child are now?"

"I received reliable information that they're in Lay-

14

ton, Florida. Joan's near her father, Dale Carlon, president of Carlon Plastics."

"A very big corporation."

"Which is why I can't take the long and arduous route of retrieving Melissa through the courts. Carlon can hire top lawyers and pay off the right people so the matter is tangled up in litigation for years."

"I take it Melissa was not to be removed from the state without the court's permission."

Clark nodded.

"I can't do anything unless you get a court order mandating custody of the child to you. That gives you legal custody even though it's subject to appeal. I don't work without proof that you *do* have legal custody."

"Sure. I waited until my lawyer told me we had a court order before coming here. I understand the risks you'd be taking."

"I want to be positive you do. The FBI and most states don't recognize that a parent can steal his own child, but if I snatch Melissa and you don't have legal custody, I might wind up in prison for kidnapping."

"And with Carlon's lawyers on me, so might I." Clark's complexion paled and his dark beard appeared darker.

"I charge twenty-five hundred dollars plus expenses," I said, "five hundred in advance."

Clark agreed to that with a curt nod. A fusillade of hail swept his side of the trailer, but he didn't seem to hear. "There won't be any . . . trouble, will there?"

"Not if I can prevent it," I said, and I meant that. "Do you have Joan's address in Layton?"

"Certainly."

"And a photograph. Recent. And a photograph of Melissa."

"I can supply those, too."

"Then when you show up here with the court order, Mr. Clark, I go to work."

Clark smiled for the second time, making it a bit better than the first.

There was a lull in the storm as well as in our conversation and no reason not to take the opportunity to leave.

Clark stood and slipped into his black rain gear. He would need the umbrella again. Though the hail had stopped, a perfectly vertical light rain fell with a gray, foreboding steadiness.

"I should be back tomorrow or the day after with the court order," Clark said as he stepped down from the trailer's threshold and opened his umbrella.

I motioned for him to wait, ducked back inside for a moment and gave him one of my cards. "Give me a call, make sure I'm here."

"Good idea," he said, tucking the card into a side pocket of his raincoat. He turned and walked to his car with an unhurried pace, refusing to make any more concessions to mere rain.

I closed the metal door, went back to the sofa and sat down. Already I could feel the heavy pulsing in my stomach that I felt every time I took a new case. Clark had asked if there might be trouble. There might always be trouble in the taking of a child from its natural mother. I didn't allow myself to dwell on the kinds of trouble that were possible.

Once I accepted Clark's money, I was committed to deal with that trouble. And I needed Clark's money.

2

He was back the next day with his court order.

I saw Clark's aging compact slow near my trailer, heard the crunch of tires on gravel and caught a glimpse of red glowing brake lights before the car passed out of my line of vision. I was doing my exercises on the concrete patio in what passes for my backyard. Having just finished my third set of deep knee bends, I was standing with my hands on my hips, waiting for my legs to stop trembling. It's not that I'm so much the physical culture type, but I'm at an age. Every day on the sports page I read about some athlete or other, washed up at thirty-six or -seven—even the great ones. That bothers me.

Gordon Clark was wearing a tailored gray suit this time, with a vest and a blood-red tucked-in tie. He was carrying an attaché case. I felt a bit shoddy in my T-shirt and sweat pants.

He smiled at me, a superior smile that said he was the superior specimen. Not that I'd argue with him. I'm big enough, and not fat, but I'm not exactly whip-cord muscle. I suspected that beneath the neat gray suit, Clark was.

"You don't look so tough," he said.

"Mr. Happy's not supposed to be tough."

"I got the court order. I was near here so I thought I'd drop it by." He opened the attache case, an expensive model with chrome trim, and handed me a piece of paper with a familiar heading.

"Okay," I said, "I'll have it copied and return it to you."

He reached into the open attaché case again, like a magician reaching into his bag of tricks, and handed

17

me out the next surprise. It was a check for five hundred dollars, closely followed by some photographs.

I walked out of the shade of the trailer to study the color snapshots. The first was of a woman, Joan Clark, leaning against what looked like a colonial pillar on a porch. She had a nifty upturned nose, close-set but large dark eyes and a small, too-curvaceous-to-be-wiry figure, one of those women who would look young even in late middle age, until the looker got close enough to notice the touches of time. The next photo was of Joan Clark and her daughter standing on the bank of a very blue lake. The daughter, Melissa, looked much like her mother, except that she was blond. And the daughter had the same innate tininess about her, the same tilt to her nose. I wondered if her mother was really blond. The third snapshot was of Melissa seated on a corner of a sofa with that characteristic knees-together, legs-straight-out pose of a seven-year-old. She had her father's smile, but with more candlepower.

"That last one of Melissa is the most recent I could find," Clark said. "It's about four months old."

I set the photos, check and court order on the metal table by my webbed lawn chair, weighting them with the heavy glass holder that contained a yellow candle that was supposed to keep mosquitoes away in the evenings.

"What's their address in Layton?" I said.

"It's three fifty-five Star Lane, on the south side of Layton. They've been there about a month. Do you want me to write it down?"

"I'll remember it, if I have to."

Clark cocked his head to the left. "What do you mean by that?"

"I mean it would be best if you flew down to Layton with me. It's the way I usually operate if I can."

He shook his head like a bull trying to shake loose a barb in the bullring. "I can't."

18

"It would be easier for the child. We wait for the right time when she's alone and simply take her with us, as if the mother knows about us."

"But I hired you so I wouldn't have to do this myself. You're supposed to be an expert. . . ." Clark shrugged helplessly, pleading to be understood. "Look, I'd like to, really. But I just can't. My job. . . . You understand. If it isn't absolutely necessary. . . ."

"As long as I have that court order and your signature on one of my contracts," I told him, "it's not necessary."

"Then I'll have to pass."

I nodded, went inside for a minute and got one of my standard contract forms and a pen. Clark read the short contract quickly and bent over the metal patio table to sign it.

"Is there any way your ex-wife could find out you hired me?" I asked.

"None at all. I haven't discussed this with anyone."

"Follow that policy," I advised him. "Surprise is important. I'll leave for Layton tomorrow, unless you have some reason for suggesting a better time."

"Tomorrow's all right with me. The sooner this thing's done, the better."

"Where can you be reached?" I asked him. "I might need to contact you, and I'll have to know where to bring Melissa when we return."

"I'm with Standard Implement." Clark reached into a gray pocket and held out an embossed white business card that proclaimed him to be a sales manager. Then he hastily drew the card back, took a pen from another pocket and scribbled his home address and phone number on the back of the card before handing it to me. His address was in a fairly expensive apartment development on the west side of the city, where expensive "executive" apartment developments were stacked on top of one another. Clark seemed to play his role as best he could with what he had.

19

"Can you tell me anything about your ex-wife that might be helpful?" I asked. "Habits, favorite activities, that sort of thing."

Clark ran his fingertips an eighth of an inch beyond the contours of his neat dark beard. "I can't think of any habits that might be helpful. Joan used to love to play tennis, though. Spent a lot of time on the court."

"Any good?"

"Good? No, but she wears down her opponents. Joan is competitive in almost everything. Aggressive. If she suspects what you're up to, your job won't be without problems."

"I'll know how to handle the situation, Mr. Clark."

He looked me up and down, as if trying to reassure himself that I could. When he turned to leave, he took two slow steps and turned back. "One thing I don't want, Nudger, is for Melissa to be hurt. Can you guarantee that she won't be?"

"I can guarantee I'll do everything to prevent it. I consider it the most important part of my job."

He stood still for a moment, then nodded, as if he'd decided I was a thorough enough professional. Then he walked toward his car.

I felt sorry for him just then. He hadn't anticipated any of this when he'd walked down the aisle and uttered his vows.

After a few more deep knee bends, I gathered up everything Clark had left with me and went inside. I phoned the airline reservation desk for space on a morning flight to Orlando. From there I would have to rent a car and drive the rest of the way to Layton.

All that remained for me to do except pack was to drive over to the post office and use their pay copier to make duplicates of the court order and the photographs Clark had given me. The original court order I would return to Clark; one copy I would place in my safe-deposit box; one copy I would take to Florida, along with Clark's signature on a copy of my contract.

In a way I was glad Clark had refused to accompany me. The father's presence didn't always make it easier on the child. Sometimes the mother put up a fuss, and the husband, out of habit or rekindled responsibility, sided with her. When that happened, I sometimes got my lumps from both of them; and usually I was re-hired to accomplish the same task, now made more difficult, a few days later. Or the woman might physically resist both of us, and she and the man would fight over the child, yanking it back and forth like so much merchandise. I had seen a few children injured seriously that way. Physically and otherwise.

The trailer's air conditioner clicked on and began to hum. The sun was asserting itself outside. I got up from where I'd been sitting, by the phone, walked into the kitchen and mixed myself a bourbon and water. My stomach didn't suit my profession. It was fluttering again with precase jitters.

I wasn't in my business because I had the nerves for it. After four years as a civilian employee of the city police department and three years as a patrolman, my superiors had come to that same unflattering conclusion. Thus began my three-year reign as local TV's Mister Happy—we dropped the "Officer" so the children would realize that policemen were much like everyone else when they weren't working—and I was the smiling cop who projected the image of Good Guy to the kids. I had always got on with the kids; just the duty for me, the higher-ups had decided. And they were right. It wasn't exactly what I'd had in mind when I joined the force, but even after three years I wasn't about to leave before I had to.

Police work was what I was trained in, and I had my contacts; so when I left the department, my choice of occupation seemed logical. At the time, anyway.

But maybe I had no right to bitch. My much maligned and misunderstood profession kept the food and liquor coming in and a tin roof over my head.

Just as the diluted bourbon was achieving its soothing influence on my nerves, the girl at the airline reservation desk phoned back and said that she'd made a mistake and asked whether I would consider a later flight that laid over in Atlanta for an hour.

I agreed to that and took an antacid tablet.

3

My flight to Orlando, via Atlanta, took off on time into a sky resembling lovingly polished fine crystal. The ground that fell away lost movement, then detail, and became a well defined, multicolored quiltwork of neat, if sometimes unsymmetrical, patterns. It was all simple from up there, where I sat behind the wing. Too bad everything didn't fall into such simple, neat patterns. Or maybe everything did, from a distance.

I settled back in the comfortable padded seat and semislept, my scant knowledge of aerodynamics balancing out my natural queasiness at flying.

Two drinks and a sampling of Southern dialect was it for the Atlanta layover, then back on the 747 and it was Georgia's red clay falling away beneath the wing. They seemed always to be constructing something in Georgia, as if only for an excuse to lay bare acres of red earth.

The plane rolled slightly to the left, altering the stark pattern of sunlight on the wing, and we headed south, proceeding toward Orlando at what seemed to be a much higher altitude.

After landing at Orlando's sun-drenched airport, I collected my baggage and made my way to a Hertz desk, where I rented a shiny new green compact. The little car was good of its kind, but there was just enough room for me and my luggage, and I had to be on the alert for pebbles and bottlecaps on the road.

I took Interstate Four out of Orlando, turned south on Twenty-seven, then drove for a while and angled west on Thirty-two, toward the Gulf Coast. Layton was twenty-five or thirty miles inland, southeast of Tampa Bay. I made the ENTERING LAYTON—POP. 3,605 sign a few minutes before five o'clock.

There was a good fishing and boating lake nearby, and Layton was close enough to the coast to have some tourist appeal. The main street was lined with motels. But off to the left I could see what had to be Layton's main industry—a huge complex of low, dark buildings set near the crest of a hill, with half a dozen tall smokestacks looming over the town like guard towers.

Disregarding the garish signs near the street, I decided one motel looked about in a league with the other, so I pulled into the lot of one called the Clover Inn, which advertised FIFTEEN DOLLARS AND UP in sun-paled flashing neon.

"Up" turned out to be twenty-two dollars, but I stretched cramped muscles and signed the register anyway. The Clover Inn had several little flat-roofed cabins spaced far enough apart to guarantee quiet at night, and it featured a clean-looking, if plain, restaurant, the Clover Grill. Besides, I couldn't face the idea of climbing back into the little green compact with the big name.

I told the man at the desk, an old guy named Eddie, that I'd be staying a few days and paid in advance. He handed me a key chained to a plastic clover engraved

23

with a numeral. Leaving the car where it was parked, I got my luggage and carried it to Number 5.

Cool air hit me when I opened the door to the boxy stucco cabin, and it felt good. I stepped inside, kicked the door shut behind me and my three-suiter, and looked around.

Nice. Restful. Light green walls, dark furniture and a bed with a thick mattress. I was satisfied with my choice.

After tossing the suitcase onto the bed, I began to unpack what I wanted to hang the wrinkles out of—a pair of slacks, pale blue shirt and a tan sport coat. I glanced at the alarm clock on the nightstand by the bed. Still plenty of daylight left, enough to take a quick shower, get something to eat at the Clover Grill and look into things. I was tired but I was working.

As I was walking across the parking lot, toward the motel restaurant, I decided to drop into the office and talk to Eddie. I could see through the window that he was alone, slouched in a leather chair near the desk, reading a magazine.

"Evening," I said as I entered the tiny paneled office.

Eddie looked up from his magazine and nodded, waiting for me to get to what I really wanted to say. He was a dehydrated old bird with a narrow face, wispy gray hair and blue eyes containing a quiet humor that life hadn't broken.

"Layton's a bigger town than I imagined," I said.

"You must not have much of an imagination. Thought you might want towels."

"Nope. Plenty of towels. How's the food in the restaurant?"

"Make you deathly ill. Don't tell 'em I said so."

"Sure." I saw that he was reading one of those factual detective magazines, with a cover featuring a bound girl in panties and bra, begging to be spared while the

24

determined type who stood over her with a ripsaw seemed to be listening to distant sirens.

"'Bout the Michigan Mutilator," he said, noticing that I'd scanned the cover. "You remember him?"

"Vaguely."

"Killed six."

"What's that big cluster of buildings east of town?" I asked.

"Used a chain saw, though. Black and Decker. That's Carlon Plastics you're talkin' about. Employs nearly half the town."

It was what I'd been afraid of. And now that I knew for sure how big Carlon Plastics was in Layton, my stomach arranged itself into a knot that would have done a scoutmaster proud. If anything did go wrong, I knew how the authorities would deal with me. Roughly and on the edge of the rules.

"What do they make up there?" I asked.

"Different things, from plastic cups for vending machines to some kind of parts for the government. There's nine more Carlon plants spread around the country, but this one was the first. Worked for 'em myself up to six years ago, in the molding section. Then I inhaled enough fumes to mess up my lungs. Had to quit, take my disability pay."

"Worth a lot to a town, an operation like that."

"Wouldn't be no town without it."

"Is there still a Carlon in the business?"

"Better believe it! Dale Carlon himself. Lives up near the plant in a ritzy place you wouldn't believe. He's the son. Father's dead."

"Carlon live alone in a place like that?"

"Yeah. Wife died nearly five years ago. No live-in servants. Got two daughters somewhere, though." He tilted his head slightly, much like the Michigan Mutilator on the magazine cover. "You here for the fishin'?"

"I wish I was. Business."

25

"Too bad. They're bitin', they say."

"Would you happen to know where Star Lane is?"

Eddie tapped the magazine on his bony knee for a while. "Not exactly," he said at last, "but I'm sure it'd be over on the south side, where there's a bunch of streets named after space stuff. You take Layton Avenue down to Palm Road, 'bout a mile from here goin' west, then you make a left an' you'll drive for a while till you see a big radio tower. You'll be in the area then. Ask somebody, they'll tell you where Star is."

The telephone rang, and with agility left over from his youth he rose and scooped up the receiver on the second ring. "No trouble," he said. "Be right there." He hung up the phone and said, "Family in Three needs towels."

"Thanks for the story on the restaurant," I told him as he came out from behind the desk and went through a folding door into another room.

I stepped back outside, into the parking lot. A huge cypress behind one of the cabins cast a dappled shadow that must have covered half the block. There was only so much daylight left. I decided to try the Clover Grill anyway.

I didn't think the food was all that bad.

Half an hour later, chewing idly on a mint-flavored toothpick, I got into the rented compact to follow old Eddie's directions to Star Lane. The evening had cooled to perfect tourist weather, and I drove with the air conditioner off and the window on the driver's side rolled down. I seemed to hit every red light, but I didn't care. Thanks to the quick dinner, I had plenty of time before sundown.

By the time I reached Palm Road it was evident that the quality of the neighborhood was declining. Motels, restaurants and quaint shops had been replaced by aging stucco apartment buildings nearer the street, taverns and pawnshops and secondhand stores.

I made my left turn onto Palm and the scenery improved, but not much. I passed some warehouses, then crossed over a tiny concrete bridge into an area of low-priced tract houses, identical but for landscaping or color. Near the top of a hill I saw the tall radio tower Eddie had mentioned, and at the next street, Planet Drive, I pulled into a cut-rate service station and got directions to Star Lane.

Two left turns and five minutes' driving got me there. Star Lane was a cul-de-sac off Star Avenue. The houses were of the same type I'd driven past for the last mile or so, with small front yards and unpaved driveways. Number 355 was a yellow frame with drawn curtains and a front picket fence in need of paint. There was no car in the driveway. I parked on the other side of the street, in front of a house with a FOR SALE sign, and sat watching.

The neighborhood seemed unpopulated except for a teenage boy four houses down, getting frustrated with an old Buick. Number 355 was quiet and humble, a rolled up newspaper near a hedge in the front yard and what looked like a folded magazine sticking from the mailbox by the door. As dusk gradually obliterated long evening shadows, I saw that there was a lamp glowing behind the thin curtains in the front window.

I didn't like the way the game was developing. Star Lane was hardly a slum, but would the daughter of the man who virtually owned the town live here with her daughter, his granddaughter? It didn't add up for me, but I knew it might add up for somebody else, to a sum I wouldn't like.

Soon the neighbors would be wondering why I was parked there, so to avoid suspicion I left and drove around for a while, returning to pass Number 355 twice. At nine forty-five there still was no sign of occupancy, no shadow of movement behind the drawn curtains, and the paper and mail were untouched.

I headed the compact back toward the motel, my uneasy feeling growing claws. At a big drugstore with a flashing neon palm tree I stopped and bought some antacid stomach tablets, a spray can of dog repellent and a bottle of blended whiskey. Dog repellent is almost as effective as Mace, and the can doesn't attract nearly the attention.

The vending machine outside the office at the Clover Inn furnished me with ice, and I mixed myself a drink and sat in my cabin, thinking about Lornee, as I usually did at some point or other when I was on a job. We'd had some fine, if precarious, years, some fine children; but when Mr. Happy was found to be having an affair with the wife of a city alderman, politics entered the somewhat muddled picture. Politics and divorce.

No one would believe that the affair was one-sided and far less serious than the press had intimated. The alderman's wife was one of those bored, self-styled eccentrics with money who'd met me when I was taking part in a local charity-celebrity function, and she had talked too much and thrown herself at me more jokingly than anything else. But the press was controlled by the rival party, and when her husband had me removed from the department, he only fanned the flames—or rather, the smoke.

I didn't contest when Lornee filed for divorce, and I thought it right to give her custody of Danny and Lynn as long as I had visitation rights. Then, a year later, Lornee left the state with a man named Hogan—a close friend of mine, a tall, lonely man who drank not a lot but a bit too much—and on a Texas highway he drove into a parked car at high speed and killed himself and my ex-wife and my children.

Nobody to blame, really. Nobody deserving of blame for that much horror; nobody, dead or alive, to take it out on, to hate. And only one survivor to harbor the memory.

Now I was lonely, the way Hogan used to be, and I was drinking, not a lot but a bit too much, the way Hogan used to drink.

Some people are star-crossed.

4

In the morning I was thankful that I hadn't dreamed. I reached out, slapped down the sharp button on the jangling alarm clock and lay for a moment in its vibrating aftermath of silence. There was a sour taste in my mouth and a numbness in my left arm where I'd lain on it in my sleep. I remembered then that I'd been on one of my alcohol-induced self-pitying binges the night before. I hated the sniveling, masochistic self-analysis to which I sometimes fell prey, hated the lethargic uselessness that often evolved from it. Every day I met people more mutilated by fate than myself. The most maudlin word in the English language is "I"—at least for me, past a certain number of drinks.

The black arrow hands on the alarm clock indicated six forty-five, the minute hand pointing toward the door in a broad hint. No time for breakfast. Just as well. As my thoughts focused on the Melissa Clark case, the familiar knot tightened in my stomach and quashed what little desire I had for food.

I managed to get my feet on the floor and commanded them to propel me to the bathroom, where I showered, shaved without nicking myself, combed my hair, and brushed my teeth with toothpaste that tasted like chalk. Gazing at my lean, somewhat lopsided features in the mirror, I wondered if my hair had started to thin. I'd be the last to know.

As soon as I was dressed I drove from the motel, in the direction of Star Lane. Halfway there I stopped at a dingy little doughnut shop built like a castle and got a cup of black coffee to go. By the time I was parked near the end of Star Lane, I'd only burned my hand twice and still had a squishy paper cup half full of coffee.

At twenty minutes to eight the first child came out, a boy of about twelve carrying a ponderous armload of books. Within a few minutes two girls, younger than the boy, emerged from the white frame house nearest my car. The girls walked to where the boy was standing, and though he carefully avoided looking at them, they stood close to him on his left. More children, mostly very young, came out of the houses on each side of the street and stood in a cluster that seemed to center around the boy with all the books.

The school bus arrived promptly at seven forty-five, big and yellow and noisy; and when it had rumbled around the corner, with more noise than speed, Star Lane was again deserted. Melissa Clark hadn't come out of the yellow house fronted by the faded picket fence.

I waited until eight o'clock. Several tired types left to go to work, and the teen-age boy I'd seen yesterday passed in his old Buick. My coffee had long since got cold. I tossed the dark liquid out the window, crumpled the cup and stuck it above the sun visor. Then I drove down the street and parked across from Number 355.

The paper was still on the lawn, the folded magazine still protruding from the mailbox. In the brightening morning there was still a faint yellow glow behind the front curtains.

I decided to be an aluminum siding salesman and

got out of the car and crossed the street. When I stepped up on the porch of Number 355 and knocked, I had the feeling I was rapping on the door of an empty house. It's an instinct anyone who's knocked on enough doors acquires.

I waited a few minutes before stepping down from the front porch and walking around to the back of the house. An old rusty swing-set frame in the far corner of the yard now supported only a bald tire suspended by a rope. The grass, where it wasn't worn away, stood about six inches high.

No one was home, I was ninety-nine percent sure, but I went up on the porch and knocked on the back door for the other one percent.

"Whad'ya want, mister?"

It was a boy of about eight, standing near the corner of the house, looking at me with the open expression of fearless curiosity possessed only by young boys and terriers.

"I'm looking for Melissa's mother. You know where she is?"

"No, sir." He was wearing a blue T-shirt about five sizes too large, and he unconsciously gripped it and stretched it down on himself almost to his knees while he stared at me.

"What's your name?" I asked in a friendly voice.

"Mick."

"How come no school today, Mick?"

"I felt bad when I woke up."

"You don't look sick."

"It's on the inside."

"How come Melissa didn't go to school?"

Mick shrugged inside his T-shirt. "Maybe she's sick, too."

"How long's it been since you've seen her?"

"Few days. She was with her mom and dad."

A scraggly-haired woman in a rumpled pink

31

housecoat stepped partway out of the back door of the house on the left. "Mick, you get back in here! If you're too sick to be in school you ain't gonna be out runnin' around!"

I smiled at her, but she didn't smile back, and I didn't like the way her hand clutched her housecoat between her breasts.

"I gotta go," Mick said.

"I would if I were you," I told him. I knocked on the back door again, loudly this time, to appear aboveboard.

That's when I saw the bullet hole.

It was from a large-caliber bullet and it was just below the doorknob, where it wasn't too noticeable. And it was neat, as if the bullet had gone through the wood from the outside.

I looked the door over and saw another neat round hole, up near the top, alongside the door frame. The bullet had made a thin groove in the frame, as if it had been fired at an angle. Stepping back on the porch, I looked over the rear of the house as if figuring a siding estimate. There was another neat bullet hole in the bottom-left corner of the window beside the back porch.

My throat went dry. I was afraid now of what might be inside the house. Squatting on the back porch, I tried to see through the lower of the two bullet holes in the door, but all I could make out was what looked like the bottom of a picture frame against the pale green of the opposite wall.

I straightened and drew a deep breath that made me light-headed for a second. Maybe the bullet holes meant nothing; maybe they'd been there for years.

Feeling a bit steadier, I went to the window and tried to peer in between the drawn curtains. They overlapped too much and it was impossible. I saw something else, though. Directly opposite the neat hole in the window pane was a neat hole in the curtain.

My breath caught in the dryness of my throat and

lumped there, and my stomach felt as if it had been stabbed with a tuning fork. There was no walking away now. It was time to have Mick's mother call the law.

They got there in five minutes and I showed them my identification and they weren't impressed. A tall man with dark hair combed like Hitler's introduced himself as Lieutenant Frank Dockard, the stocky uniformed policeman with him as Sergeant Avery. By their manner I saw within a few minutes that Avery was the silent servant and that Dockard fashioned himself the brains.

Mick and his mother watched soberly from their front porch as I told my story, and Dockard made notes in a leather-covered note pad with the diligence of a monk copying an ancient manuscript. When I was finished, he snapped the note pad shut and gave no indication of what he thought, and the professionally placid, thick features of Sergeant Avery were unchanged.

After a while Dockard rubbed a long forefinger behind his right ear, as if checking for an injury. "Let's take a look at these bullet holes," he said, and led the way toward the back of the house.

The three of us stood on the back porch while Mick and his mother looked silently on from next door. Dockard grunted when he saw the holes in the door, stepped down off the porch and grunted again when he saw the bullet hole in the window and the corresponding hole in the curtain.

"Phoned Mr. Carlon," Dockard said as Avery inserted a pencil into the bullet holes to check the angles of the shots. "He said he hasn't heard from his daughter in months but knew she wasn't in Layton."

"If he hasn't heard from her in months," I said, "how can he know where she is?"

"He can know where she isn't."

33

I decided not to rise to that bait. I got a roll of antacid tablets from my pocket and popped one of the white disks into my mouth.

"What's that for?" Dockard asked.

"Nervous stomach."

He looked me over appraisingly with small brown eyes. "Can't blame you for that."

I could feel the veiled suspicion, the catlike waiting to pounce on my first wrong move, my first indication of whatever they thought I was trying to pull off.

"Look," I said to Dockard, "I'm only doing my job. We're in the same business. . . . You ought to understand that."

"I don't understand what a Carlon and her daughter would be doing living in a little dump like this, especially here in Layton. And I don't know if I like your line of business, either. It's legalized kidnapping."

"So is what Joan Clark did. The father has as much right to the child as she does. Besides, after I make the snatch I always let the child decide."

"Decide what?"

"Whether to go or stay."

"And what do they do?"

"After we talk it out they usually pick the parent who cared enough about them to hire me."

"And if they don't?"

"I leave them and refund my client's fee. It's in the fine print of my contract."

"That's stupid business."

"It doesn't happen very often. I'm a persuasive talker."

Avery was finished fooling around with the bullet holes.

"Why don't we go in?" I asked, but I was afraid to go in and Dockard could see that.

"Better the front way," he said, and we walked around the house. We must have been driving Mick and his mother crazy.

The front door was locked, and at a nod from Dockard, Avery leaned his bulk against it and the latch splintered from the wood frame. My heart tried to scramble up my throat as we went in.

The inside of the tiny house was uncomfortably hot, stuffy, with the thick stillness of a place that has been closed tight for a long time. We were in the living room—red shag carpet, worn sofa, recliner chair, incongruously expensive stereo set up along one wall. The lamp on the table by the front window was still glowing.

None of us said anything. The kitchen was right off the living room; I could see a corner of the green refrigerator. As we walked toward the doorway, a peculiar odor, as of something putrescent, struck me, and my legs began to tremble. The kitchen doorway seemed farther away.

There was no one in the kitchen. One of the chrome-legged chairs was on its side near the stove. On the table a horde of gnats swarmed about the rotting remains of a carryout chicken dinner in a red and white cardboard bucket.

The wood on the inside of the door had splintered away from the bullet holes. The two bullets fired through the door had lodged in the wall above the sink; the shot fired through the window had left a bullet somewhere inside a cupboard containing a jumble of aluminum pots and pans. Silent Sergeant Avery pointed a square-tipped finger at something lying on the white porcelain surface of the ledge of the sink. It was a woman's ring, a ruby surrounded by a circle of diamonds in a gold setting. A jeweler's appraisal wasn't needed to see that its value reached the thousands.

"Keeh-rist!" Dockard said with appropriate respect for wealth. He bent closely over the ring but didn't touch it.

35

"It might be worth more than the house," I observed.

"I'm going to make a phone call," Dockard said, straightening. "You two wait for me outside."

Within fifteen minutes Dale Carlon arrived in a long gray Mercedes. He got out of the parked car with a minimum of effort, as if he'd rehearsed the move. As he strode toward where we stood in the front yard, I took in the perfectly styled gray hair above even, masculine features, the elegant cut of the gray suit with vest, the wet-looking shine on the expensive black shoes. He was well-groomed; he was flawless. He was the department store's distinguished mannequin struck to life.

"Is this the man?" he said to Dockard without glancing at me.

"Yes, sir," Dockard said. "Alo Nudger is his name."

"Let's see the ring."

Almost before Carlon had asked, Docker's hand shot forward, palm up, with the glinting ring catching the best of the sun.

"It's Joan's," Carlon said without hesitation. "It was a graduation gift." He looked at me now with angular gray eyes. "What do you know about my daughter?" he asked in a level voice.

"That she was living here with your granddaughter."

"I don't expect you to understand this," Carlon said, "but that's rather hard for me to believe. I'm told Gordon Clark hired you."

"Yes, sir." I found myself calling him sir, too. It irritated me. "He's the one who gave me this address."

"I don't doubt that Joan was here," Carlon said to Dockard, "or someone who knows something about Joan. I want the neighbors questioned about the occupants of this house."

"Yes, sir."

Behind Dockard a dented blue Chevy pulled into the driveway next door, and a middle-aged woman and

36

a girl of about seven got out. The woman reached awkwardly into the backseat and straightened up with a brown paper grocery bag. We had caught the girl's attention, and she slipped through the fence where one of the pickets was loose and came running across the yard toward us.

"Grampa!"

The stout middle-aged woman came around the fence and in through the gate, a curious, half-fearful expression on her heart-shaped face.

I saw the smile and the pertly uptilted nose on the little girl, who could only be Melissa Clark. She flew at Dale Carlon with perfect trust, and he bent, hugged her once and kissed her.

"I'm Mrs. Kimmel," the woman said with a nervous smile that pleaded for friendship.

"What are you doing with my granddaughter?" Carlon asked smoothly.

"Are you Joan's father?"

"I am."

Mrs. Kimmel's smile lost its nervousness and gained warmth. "Joan's husband was away for a few days, and she wanted me to baby-sit Melissa while she visited an aunt who's ill in Orlando."

I held out one of the snapshots Gordon Clark had given me. "Is this the woman who lives here?"

Mrs. Kimmel shifted her bag of groceries and looked at the photograph. "Why, yes . . . of course."

I turned to show the photograph to Carlon, but he didn't look at it. He didn't have to. Melissa and the ring constituted all the proof he needed. He was standing still, one hand unconsciously caressing the seven-year-old's slender neck as she clung to his leg. I didn't know if he looked more worried or thoughtful. When he spoke, his voice had lost its aloof assurance.

"Joan doesn't have an aunt in Orlando," he said. "Or a husband anywhere."

37

5

We drove toward the Layton police headquarters. I sat in the front seat of the plain tan sedan, next to the driver, Avery. Dockard sat in back, directly behind me; he was silent, but I could almost hear his brain whirring. Dale Carlon drove ahead of us in his sleek Mercedes, as if forging the way.

The headquarters building was a low, beige-brick structure with several tall antennas jutting from its flat roof. It was set on a wide green lawn, neatly landscaped with low-lying shrubbery, and I could see several parked patrol cars on a blacktopped lot behind the building. Avery held the door open for us and we entered, walked past a grandmotherly receptionist-switchboard operator and down a sterile-tiled hall to an unmarked door. A scrub-faced, somber patrolman went in with Carlon and Dockard. Avery stayed behind, held open the unmarked door for me with polite instructions to wait inside.

Alone in the tiny room, I sat in a straight-backed wooden chair by a small varnished table and slipped an antacid tablet into my mouth. I chewed the tablet frantically, realized I was getting carried away and took a few deep breaths to relax.

I looked around. The room was practically unfurnished—bare floor, single dirty window with broken venetian blinds, only the one small wooden table with three matching chairs and a dented and sloppily repainted file cabinet set against one pale green wall. I didn't like the room.

An hour passed. I knew they were making me wait on purpose, trying to wear down my nerve. They couldn't know there wasn't much need for that. An automobile horn sounded in the distance, and there were muffled voices as several people passed nearby; but all that was visible outside the streaked glass of the single window were the leafy branches of a large tree. The little room smelled of perspiration and fear, and some of it was mine.

Finally Dockard entered the room with Avery at his elbow. Both men appeared tired.

"Sorry to keep you waiting," Dockard lied.

"That's all right," I lied back. "I had fun looking out the window."

He nodded in admiration at the brave front and sat down across from me in one of the straight-backed chairs. Avery remained standing, a stoic figure.

"I'd like your complete story on tape, if you have no objections," Dockard said.

"Am I being officially held for questioning in the girl's disappearance?"

Dockard raised his eyebrows. "Of course not. We thought we had your cooperation. Aren't we in the same business?"

"The same," I said. I knew how it would be if I failed to cooperate, with the missing girl's father owning the town and the police department. Not that I minded cooperating in a straight game, but this was hardly that.

Dockard smiled and rested his hands on the varnished tabletop in a passive gesture, and Avery walked to the dented file cabinet and took a recorder from the top drawer. I had the notion to request a lawyer, but wasn't that the request of a guilty man? And if Carlon owned the law, no doubt he owned the lawyers.

Avery set the recorder, a flat Japanese model, on the table in front of me, and Dockard switched it on, then sat back in his chair expectantly, as if he'd just done something wonderful. I cleared my throat and began to talk.

It took me close to half an hour to explain to the recorder how I'd reached my present predicament, starting with the arrival of Gordon Clark at my house trailer and ending with the arrival of the police at 355 Star Lane. Every so often Dockard would interrupt me with questions that didn't seem very pertinent, but even so, I could almost hear the clang of my cell door.

An elderly secretary came in with three large ceramic mugs of coffee on a tray, set the tray on the table next to the humming Japanese recorder and left. Dockard slid one of the mugs across the table to me and turned off the recorder. He spooned sugar and powdered cream into his steaming cup and held up the containers in an offering gesture to me. I declined and took a sip of the strong black coffee, almost hot enough to peel the skin from my lips.

"Does this story jell with the facts?" Dockard asked me confidentially.

"I wouldn't have been so cooperative if it didn't."

He pursed his lips at that. We both knew I'd had no choice.

Avery shifted his weight to his heels and crossed his arms. I'd almost forgotten he was there.

"I'm telling you this because I feel duty bound," Dockard said, "while you still have a chance to change your story. I don't know if you're exactly aware of who Dale Carlon is, but he's the last man for miles around who you'd choose to cross."

"I don't choose to cross anybody," I said. "All I was trying to do was my job, returning Melissa Clark to her father."

"Maybe she belongs with her mother."

". . . Who happens to be Dale Carlon's daughter."

There was a narrowing of his brown eyes without change of facial expression. "It's not like anybody owns this department, Nudger."

40

It's not like it, I thought, *it is it.*

Dockard waited patiently for me to answer, then gave up.

"You mind waiting around while this is transcribed?" he asked finally, slipping the cassette from the recorder.

"Not at all."

He stood and thanked me; then he and Avery walked from the room, leaving half open the door to the hall. As a snub? A dare? I leaned back and sipped coffee that was cool enough now for human consumption.

It was easier to pass the time now that I could hear part of what was going on outside the room—the clatter of a teletype from across the hall, its rhythm broken by the occasional thumping of an electric typewriter; the voices of two men passing the time, talking shop, now and then getting into the subject of the eastern division pennant race. Neither of them knew much baseball.

"Here's something on Branly," one of them suddenly said, interrupting the other's sermon on the virtues of a good defensive shortstop. "According to neighbors, he and his wife and kid lived at the Star Lane address for a little over a month."

"Is the wife the Carlon bitch?"

"So the neighbors say."

"Think they were really married?"

"Who gives a damn anymore?"

"Marion of the Saint Louis Cardinals was the best ever."

Wagner of Pittsburgh, I thought, sitting back in my chair, *and he could hit. . . . So Branly, whoever he may be, is the other man.* I remembered now that Mick, of the saggy T-shirt, had mentioned something about seeing Melissa with her mother and father. This Branly complicated things.

41

I sat quietly, straining for more information, but all I got was baseball misinformation. *Who wanted a short-stop who couldn't hit?*

What was left of my coffee was cold when Dockard came back into the room as if he'd only stepped out a minute ago. I was surprised to see Gordon Clark behind the detective.

Clark stepped into the room and gave me a quick, humorless smile. "Mr. Nudger." He looked bedraggled, and there was slack flesh beneath his reddened eyes. His brown suit was rumpled, and his dark beard was slightly flattened on one side, as he he'd slept on it. I guessed he'd been airborne for the past several hours.

"This him, Mr. Clark?" Dockard asked.

"He's the man I hired."

"Things took an unexpected turn," I said. "I'm sorry."

"I should have come down here with you as you suggested," Clark said.

"That wouldn't have changed anything."

"Nudger's right about that, Mr. Clark," Dockard said. He floated a hand to Clark's shoulder to lead him from the room.

"I'm at the Clover Inn, on Main Drive," I said to Clark.

He nodded as he left the room. Dockard stayed behind.

"He verified your story," Dockard said.

"Then if you don't mind, I've done enough cooperating for the day."

Dockard grinned, opened the door. "Come into my office, Nudger."

It was more than a simple invitation. I got up wearily and followed him down the hall to let him hold open another door for me.

Dockard's office was large, or at least it seemed so to

42

me after my confinement in the tiny interrogation room. There was a nice walnut desk, pictures on the walls and a soft vinyl chair for me to sit in. The chair was best of all.

"Tired?" Dockard asked, sitting behind his desk and lighting a cigarette.

I didn't think it was a question that deserved an answer.

"Things have gotten even muckier than you think," Dockard said.

I wasn't surprised to hear him say that. The whole affair had taken on a certain inevitable feel, evoking in me the same foreboding that must brush the senses of someone gradually approaching the vortex of a whirlpool.

"Joan Clark and her daughter were living with a man named David Branly," Dockard said, attempting to blow a smoke ring and creating something closer to a mushroom. "Know anything about him?"

"Only that he's lived with Joan and Melissa Clark on Star Lane for a little over a month. I overheard that here earlier." I wondered if I'd been meant to overhear, so Dockard could observe my reaction from some hidden vantage point on the other side of one of the tiny room's walls. "Wasn't I meant to eavesdrop?"

Dockard neither confirmed nor denied. "He's dead," he said.

I considered that a hell of a way to change the subject. My stomach dropped a few notches. "You mean Branly?"

Dockard nodded, lifting a hand to brush back his Hitlerian lock of hair. "Mr. Branly was found dead yesterday in a car parked behind a Laundromat on Surf Avenue."

"And not of natural causes?"

"A twelve-gauge shotgun sawed down to less than eighteen inches was fastened with electrician's tape to

43

the steering wheel column of his car, down low near the floor, where he wouldn't see it. It was aimed up the column, straight through the center of the steering wheel, and a wire ran from the trigger to a lever attached to the accelerator pedal. When Branly stepped down on the pedal to start the car. . . ." Dockard spread his hands, palms down.

In spite of myself I imagined what Branly must have felt—the shock, perhaps the instantaneous knowledge and horror at the blast of flame and noise at his feet.

"He was struck in the stomach and groin," Dockard went on. "Killed instantly."

"Mixed up with an organization, maybe?"

Dockard shrugged. "If it was a gangland killing, this is the first time I've heard of this method being used. Generally these things follow a pattern, and generally they don't happen in Layton." Dockard drew open his flat center drawer, reached in and tossed several glossy photographs on the desk before me.

I tried to swallow my squeamishness, forced myself to pick up the photos and look.

They were Branly's death photos, but they were surprisingly undisturbing to my stomach. The pictures showed a fairly young man from the waist up who appeared to be sleeping and experiencing a bad dream. There were several front shots and two with the head turned for a profile angle. It was a classically handsome profile. Branly was still wearing a plain sport coat and loose-knotted tie, and the only indication of violence was some splatters of blood marring the pattern of the coat. I tried not to think of how the area of the body below the bottom edges of the photographs must look.

"I've never seen him before," I said, laying the photographs back on the desk.

"Neighbors of the Star Lane house have. When they saw those photographs, they identified him immediately as that nice young Mr. Branly. And they identified Joan Clark as Mrs. Branly. Said they were a pleasant young couple, not outgoing, though. Said they moved in just over a month ago and led a quiet life."

"What prompted you to ask the Star Lane neighbors about Branly?"

"The car he was found dead in had out-of-state registration—under Joan Clark."

I sighed, rested my palms on my knees and felt their warm moisture through the material of my pants. "Lieutenant Dockard, if I could help in any way, I would. What I am is a man trying to make a living, and I don't mind telling you I'm into something here I don't want to be into. I never heard of David Branly until today, and I don't like being involved in the investigation of his murder. All I know about any of it is what I've already told you."

Dockard ground out his cigarette stub in a glass ashtray, slowly and carefully, as if it were something alive and he savored the killing of it. The last hazy wisp of smoke had drifted up from the ashtray and dissipated before he looked at me again.

"I believe you, Nudger," he said, "but I don't disallow the fact that I might be wrong. We don't railroad people here in Layton, but you've got to understand that this is an unusual case, an important case to everyone involved." He stood to signify that it was at last time for me to leave.

"Because Carlon is a big man?"

"We both know that's why," Dockard admitted, "and we both know that's the reason certain rules and procedures might be stepped over, or on, in this investigation. If we don't come up with something within a reasonable length of time, there'll be repercussions, so everyone connected with the case wants results."

"What I want is to be out of it."

"Maybe you can be, Nudger. Your car's parked in the lot out back."

I stood up stiffly, almost reluctantly, from the soft vinyl chair, crossed the thick carpet to the door.

Walking from Dockard's office was pure pleasure, equaled only by the pleasure of walking from the building.

My humble motel cabin beckoned like home.

6

I steered the green compact into the Clover Inn's gravel parking lot, listening to the tiny stones pinging off the insides of the fenders. Afternoon shadows were lengthening, and I saw that the parking space in front of cabin 5 was in shade.

After I parked and switched off the ignition, the little car's engine turned over a few times on its own, as if overheated. I felt overheated myself. Today brought me closer than I wanted to get to becoming involved in a murder case. The problem with homicides was that there was always someone else involved who was a murderer. All my frayed nerves needed was the knowledge that someone might be stalking me—with my death in mind. I didn't kid myself. I knew it was better to be a dead hero than a live coward. It was just that I didn't have the stomach for it. I lived on.

I struggled out of the car and stretched, realizing abruptly that I was hungry. After a cool shower to make me alive again, I'd eat at the Clover Grill, then phone for reservations on the first flight I could board out of Orlando.

When I entered the cabin, I found Dale Carlon sitting on the bed.

"Afternoon, Mr. Nudger."

I closed the door behind me, wishing I hadn't bothered to come back for my luggage. Carlon was smiling at me—a new side of him. It was an even, handsome, definitely PR smile.

"How did you get in here?" I asked.

"It happens that indirectly I own part of this motel, Mr. Nudger." The smile turned genuine. "You'll find that few doors are locked to me here in Layton."

I was momentarily angry with myself for feeling uncomfortable, awed by his authority. "That brings us around to why you're here," I said.

"I thought you'd like to know you've accomplished your objective. Melissa is returning home with her father on the earliest direct flight. Gordon and I decided it would be better this way until things are settled."

"Maybe I can be on the same flight," I said. I considered offering him a drink, then decided my brand would probably fall below his standards. To hell with it.

"I hope not, Mr. Nudger. I want to hire you."

That took me aback, but it explained why he'd been waiting for me. "As you said, I've already accomplished my objective." I wondered if he was letting Gordon Clark take Melissa because he wanted to or because he knew he'd have to eventually anyway. Or would he have, here in Layton?

The handsome smile grew more confident. "I'm sure I can change your mind."

I knew what he was getting around to. "Why do you want to hire me, Mr. Carlon?"

"To find my daughter."

I walked to the small writing desk, half leaned, half

47

sat on it. "Your daughter is mixed up in murder, Mr. Carlon. I don't want to be. I don't extend my investigative activities that far, but I can give you the names of some top investigators who'd be interested."

"I'd like you to make an exception in my case."

"I'm afraid of murder, Mr. Carlon."

"Would fifty thousand dollars for your services make you less afraid?"

I sat down all the way on the small writing desk and looked at him. He was serious—more than that, sure of himself.

"Not less afraid," I said, "only wealthier. Why would you be willing to pay me that much when you can hire better investigators for a small fraction of the cost?"

With thumb and index finger he smoothed a crease in the leg of his elegant suit. "I have much to lose by unfavorable public exposure of any kind, Mr. Nudger. You're already into the case by accident, as it were, and you've seen some of the dirty linen that I don't wish made public. Since you've seen some, I prefer that you, rather than another unnecessary party, see whatever else must be seen. That way I have only you to trust and not you and someone else. And as your client you owe me at least a modicum of confidentiality. The fifty thousand dollars is for your secrecy as well as your services."

Fear fought greed while Carlon watched with the air of a man who'd seen the battle often.

"A good deal of money," he commented, rooting for his side.

"I'm known for my avarice, Mr. Carlon."

"I see you as practical."

I laughed inside at that, even as I cringed. I already knew what I'd decided, against every instinct but greed.

"This will have to be a handshake deal, Mr. Nudger,

48

without written records of any kind. Ten thousand now, forty thousand when Joan is located or returned to me. And of course I'll pay your expenses." Without averting his gaze he reached into an inside pocket and withdrew a thick stack of green bills, not in an envelope but rubber-banded together. A bit of psychology there. Good psychology. "I won't require a receipt, Mr. Nudger, as a gesture of our mutual trust."

That was meaningless, we both knew. Where could I hide from him if I did decide to run with the ten thousand?

I stood away from the writing desk. With my left hand I accepted the bills, with my right I shook Carlon's dry hand. I detected a very subtle change in his attitude, a confirmation in his eyes. He had judged me correctly.

"I think you'll find," he said, "that my influence can help in your investigation by opening many doors."

"I don't doubt that," I said, glancing at my own door.

"Now, Nudger, where do you intend to start?" Carlon adopted a much more familiar bearing now that he'd bought me, as if any moment he might slip off his shoes and stretch out on the bed.

"I'd like to know where Gordon Clark is."

"Gordon? Why?"

"Because I need to talk to Melissa."

I could see the hesitancy move through his body. He didn't like being probed in a soft spot, and Melissa was that. "Surely there's no need to bring her into this, not at this point."

"She spent the last several months with your daughter, Mr. Carlon. The missing months."

He stared hard at me, trying to read something in my face. "She's only seven. . . ."

"I'll know how to talk to her."

He saw in me what he wanted, and nodded.

"They're at the Dolphin Motel in Orlando. Their flight leaves at seven tonight."

Carlon gave me the motel's phone number and his own private number. Then he left, without the ten thousand he'd brought.

Seven o'clock. To get to Orlando in time to talk to Melissa, I'd have to put off eating again.

Thanks to Carlon, I wasn't hungry now anyway.

7

I was on the outskirts of Orlando by five that evening, and by five fifteen I was listening to the measured ticking of my directional signal while waiting to make a left off a wide four-lane street to park in front of the Dolphin Motel. The drive had taken longer than I'd planned. A brief late-afternoon shower had slowed highway traffic, and though the sun was out brightly again, there were still a few clear droplets and streaks of rainwater on the compact's windshield and gleaming green hood.

The Dolphin Motel was one of those neat and moderately priced family motels, two stories high and built in a wide, sweeping U around a fenced-in swimming pool. The pool was crowded now with a few adults and a proliferation of the preteen and very young, leaping and splashing with unfeigned ecstasy, as though it would never be over. Near the office I walked past a large sheet-metal dolphin that was lurching repeatedly in clumsy mimicry of that species' graceful arcs through ocean waves. There was a self-satisfied, silly grin on what passed for its face.

Gordon and Melissa Clark were in Number 27, second floor, toward the rear of the motel. I climbed metal steps to an iron-railed cement walkway, stepping aside for another flock of small children. The motel was no doubt packed with families here for the illusory adventure of Disney World. For a moment the memories began to bloom at the back of my mind, and I reminded myself of why I was here.

Gordon Clark opened the door immediately at my knock. He looked fresher than he had at police headquarters. The redness was gone from his eyes and he wore neatly creased plaid pants and a blue short-sleeved sport shirt open at the neck. He invited me in and stepped back.

The room was motel modern—two single beds, angular low furniture and a ceiling fixture that resembled a space satellite. Melissa was sitting cross-legged on the floor, near the foot of one of the beds, piecing together a small jigsaw puzzle. Good practice for her, the way her life was going.

"I'm sorry about how things turned out," I told Clark.

"It wasn't your fault. And I have Melissa." He turned toward her. "Melissa, this is Mr. Nudger."

She glanced up from the puzzle. "He has to shave."

I crossed the room and sat on the edge of the bed nearer her. "I've decided never to shave again. I'm going to grow a long beard and tuck it into my belt."

She looked at me and smiled slightly. "How long will that take?"

"Few days."

Melissa put down her puzzle piece. She was ready to argue about that. "Dave didn't shave once all weekend and his beard wasn't that long."

"Must be something wrong with his beard. Who's Dave?"

51

"Mommy's friend."

"I came here to talk to you about your mommy."

"She's gone."

"Do you know where?"

"She said she'd be back."

"Did you like living on Star Lane?"

Melissa shrugged and stared down at the half-completed puzzle, a striped kitten jumping over something not yet pieced together.

"It was bigger than your other house, wasn't it?" I asked before she could get interested again in the puzzle. But she was only staring at it for a focal point.

"No," she said, "the other house was bigger, with lots more people in it."

"Where was the other house?"

"On a street with tall houses on it. It was a 'parment."

"An apartment building?"

"Uh-huh."

"In Layton?"

"Uh-uh." She shook her head no.

"Where at?"

"On a street with other tall houses on it."

"How far away?"

"Long ways."

She picked up a puzzle piece from the carpet, held it with her little finger extended, as if she were holding toast spread with jam.

"Did you like Dave?" I asked.

"Most times. . . ." she answered absently.

"That one goes there, doesn't it?" I said, helping her fit the piece into the puzzle to complete one of the kitten's forepaws. I was given a smile of gratitude. "Did you like living at the apartment best?"

"No, there were people all the time. Mommy and Vic always had people there, talking 'stead of sleeping."

"Who's Vic?" I asked Melissa, glancing at Gordon Clark, who looked stupefied.

"You know. . . ."

"A friend of Dave's?"

She laughed, picked up another puzzle piece.

"A friend of your mom's?"

"Yes."

"What did all these people talk about when they came to your apartment and you were trying to sleep?"

"Ingerence. Other things sometimes, too."

"I don't know what ingerence is, Melissa."

"Well, that's what they talked about. Mom and Vic talked about it all the time, too."

"Did Dave?"

She laughed again. "You're silly."

"Was your mother happy on Star Lane with Dave?"

She seemed to consider, her wide eyes looking inward. "She was worried all the time."

"Did they ever argue?"

"Uh-huh. The time when Vic didn't shave."

"What did they fight about?"

"I dunno." She had about reached her limit of conversing with me and was being drawn back to the challenge of the puzzle. I leaned down again, helping her fit the pieces.

"Did your mom like Vic better than Dave?"

She giggled as she completed the red ball beneath the kitten.

"Vic and Dave are the same person, aren't they?" I said.

"Course."

"Where did you live before the apartment building?"

"Someplace the same. I'm hungry, Dad."

"We'll eat in a little while, Melissa," Gordon Clark said.

I stood up from the bed. "Thanks for talking to me, Melissa."

"I'm hungry now."

"Okay, honey," Clark said, "in just a little while."

He and I stepped outside on the bright cement walkway.

"Did talking to her help you any?" he asked.

"I know more than I did."

Clark slipped his hands into his pants pockets and stood with his shoulders back, as if to expose himself to the maximum amount of sunlight. "Why do you think this Branly guy called himself Vic?"

I glanced down at the kids yelling and thrashing their way through cool water in the pool. "We'll know that when we find out why he was killed."

"And why Joan's disappeared?"

I nodded. "Why everything." I watched him half close his eyes to the sun. "Do you think Joan might come back to you?"

"No, but I'll let you know if she does." Clark smiled his curiously dreary smile, shook my hand. "I'll mail you the second part of your fee."

"That won't be necessary," I told him. "I didn't earn it." As I heard myself speak, I was amazed at the generosity rooted in my newfound wealth.

"I have Melissa back."

"You probably would have got her back without me."

He slipped the fingertips of his right hand back into his pocket. "I feel I should warn you about something, Nudger."

"Go ahead," I told him. "I have so much to worry about now, it probably won't make much difference."

"In confidence, of course."

"Of course."

"I don't think you should trust your client all the way."

I waited for him to tell me why. He chose not to, so I nodded and thanked him for the word of caution. He was Dale Carlon's son-in-law; he should know.

When Clark opened the door to go inside, Melissa

54

peered out from the comparative dimness of the motel room.

"Come back when you have your beard," she said.

I decided to have dinner at a western-style steak house in Orlando before driving back to Layton. As I ate the surprisingly good rib-eye and baked potato, I thought over my conversation with Melissa. She was a typically succinct and scatterbrained seven-year-old, and though our talk had brought out a few hard facts, I suspected that what she'd given me were puzzle pieces much like the ones she'd held in her hands. Why did Branly use two first names? Where was the apartment in which they'd lived? Who were the people who had visited them often? And what the hell was "ingerence"?

By the time I reached dessert I knew which way I'd have to go in the investigation. Melissa hadn't given me a starting point, so it would have to be the dead David Branly. *He* was easy enough to keep tabs on, and the Layton police should have had some background information on him by now. If I probed about in that area of time just before his death and traced his movements, I was bound to learn something of the recent activities of Joan Clark. The trouble was that Branly's murderer was also a part of that area of time, making it a dangerous area in which to be probing about.

The house on Star Lane would be the place to start, and with Dale Carlon's influence the Layton police should be completely cooperative.

I finished my ranch-house pudding and signaled a cowgirl for a refill on the coffee. It was going to be a long drive back to Layton.

8

Gaining access to the Star Lane house was no problem, involving only a phone call to Dale Carlon, who offered to meet me there the next day with the key.

In the morning, again using Carlon's influence, I phoned Dockard at the Layton police headquarters from my cabin at the Clover Inn and asked him what had been turned up on the Branly killing.

"To date, nothing much," Dockard said. "The ME tells us Branly died in his late twenties, perfectly healthy except for all those shotgun pellets. Nothing on the gun yet, either. Wiped clean of prints. You know how impossible it is to trace a shotgun. It's an Ithaca twelve-gauge semi-automatic with the stock and barrel sawed down. A fairly expensive gun, about seven years old, according to the company's check of the serial number."

"Making it all the harder to trace. Anything found in the house that might help?"

"We combed it fine; there's nothing there, but you're welcome to look for yourself if you want."

As long as Carlon's behind me, I thought. "What about Branly's fingerprints? You should be able to get some specific information about him through them."

Dockard's tone was tolerant. "His prints aren't on file. Apparently he was never in the service and hasn't got a record."

I thanked the lieutenant and hung up. The fact that Branly had no record was in itself interesting. It made the possibility of his having been killed in a gangland assassination all the more unlikely.

There was little comfort for me in that unlikelihood. The lone and unpredictable killer frightened me more

56

than the underworld hit man. If I had to be murdered, I wanted it done by a professional. Anything to reduce the possibility of prolonged pain.

I shook my head and called myself a few derogatory but accurate names. After setting my watch by the clock on the nightstand, I left for my appointment with Carlon at the Star Lane house.

I was ten minutes early but Carlon was there, waiting in front of 355 Star Lane in his gray Mercedes. When he saw me drive up in the green compact, he got out of his car and came toward me. He was dressed in a tailor-made, very expensive navy-blue suit that was as out of place on Star Lane as was his Mercedes. I, on the other hand, fit right in.

Carlon nodded a hello to me, then handed me a house key. "You might as well keep it, Nudger."

"Okay," I said, "let's go see if it works."

I unlocked the front door and we stepped inside, onto the red shag carpet. The atmosphere was hot and stifling, and I had the same claustrophobic feeling that I'd experienced entering the house the first time, with Dockard and Avery. There was even an aftertaste of fear.

"My God!" Carlon said. "Don't they have any air conditioning?" He spotted a thermostat and went for it, pushing something that brought a click, a rattling hum and supposedly cool air.

I walked around the living room slowly, then went into the kitchen. The rotting remains of the carryout chicken dinner had been removed. The slugs had been dug from the wall, and presumably, the bullet in the cupboard had been located and removed. Everything else seemed unmoved, as if I were looking at a photograph for the second time. The chrome-legged chair still lay on its side on the linoleum, and I saw that the kitchen wastebasket still contained litter.

"The landlord's being compensated to keep hands off for a while," Carlon explained behind me.

I opened the green refrigerator, found a still-sealed quart of milk, a few condiment jars and some bologna going bad on the top shelf. The refrigerator clicked on to add its hum to the air conditioner's, and I closed the door.

"Do you really expect to find something here that the police missed?" Carlon asked.

"Not necessarily, but I might interpret something differently."

He faded back into the living room. After checking out the kitchen, looking inside cupboards and drawers, under shelf paper, behind the stove and then through the litter in the wastebasket, I joined him.

"Find anything?" he asked.

"Only what you'd expect after somebody moved out on a few hours' notice." I went to check the bedrooms.

The first bedroom must have been Melissa's. There were a few toys lying about, some brightly covered books and some threadbare dresses in the closet. The dresser drawers contained only the usual assortment of underclothes and some blankets. Decals of cartoon characters covered the wall behind the bed, and their happy, zany expressions seemed out of place in the otherwise drab room.

The other bedroom had been Branly and Joan's, a pale blue room furnished cheaply and sparsely. There was little sign of Joan there—a pink hairbrush on the dresser top with a few dark hairs caught in its bristles, an empty perfume bottle and a pair of high-heeled shoes with one of the heels broken. There were more of Branly's effects in the bedroom, but they were curiously impersonal. A suit and three shirts in the closet—pockets empty—and some socks and underwear in one of the dresser drawers. I could almost imagine Joan Clark removing anything that might pertain to his identity before she left. Sadly enough, she seemed to have forgotten nothing.

I checked empty drawers, the tops of closet shelves; I even peered under the bed. With no results. On the floor, near the bed, were a couple paperback books—a Gothic romance and a self-help book on salesmanship, both worn and dog-eared. I turned the books binding-up and thumbed through the pages in the hope of finding something wedged there, but nothing fell out. Maybe Branly had been a salesman, or maybe the books had been left in the house by a previous tenant. I walked back into the living room, disgusted with my lack of progress, my stomach churning just from being in the small and depressing house.

"It seems to me you're wasting valuable time here, Nudger," Carlon said, standing with his hands locked behind him as he stared out the front window.

"There was only one way to know for sure," I said, reaching for my roll of antacid tablets. I fumbled, trying to pry the top disk loose from the silver foil, and the roll of tablets squirted from my fingers and bounced across the carpet, not getting very far in the thick red shag. When I bent to pick up the roll, I saw something that made me forget my immediate need for a tablet.

The house had apparently been decorated just before Branly and Joan had moved in; the woodwork was freshly enameled. But near the kitchen doorway, where the telephone sat on a small table, I saw a set of numerals scratched on the underside of the flawlessly enameled molding that ran along the wall, four feet above the floor. I moved nearer and examined the phone number more closely.

"This number mean anything to you?" I asked Carlon, then read off the numerals.

But he hadn't heard me. He was staring, as if fascinated, at a newspaper on the sofa. I walked over and saw that the paper was folded to the story and photo of a man named Robert Manners, a Los Angeles business executive who had committed suicide due to the pressures of his job. He'd jumped from the high roof of his office building, and a photographer had caught his image on the way down, arms and legs outspread, tie trailing like an aviator's scarf, coattails of an expensive dark suit—one like Carlon's—standing straight out in the rushing wind. I wondered how much contentment Carlon's money had really bought him. Then I recited the phone number again and he gave a little start and focused his attention on me.

"I'm unfamiliar with the number," he said. "Where did you find it?"

"It was freshly scratched on the woodwork near the phone. There's a writing pad and pencil by the phone, so it could be that whoever scratched this number considered it very important. A piece of paper can get lost a lot easier than a piece of woodwork."

"That makes obvious sense, to a point," Carlon said. "How could the police have overlooked it?" There was an edge to his voice, the voice of a man uncompromising toward incompetence.

"It wasn't meant to be found. I'd have missed it myself but for the good fortune of being clumsy." Why was I sticking up for Dockard?

"I don't see any reasonable excuse," Carlon said. "The number was in the house; it should have been found."

He was right, but it was a waste of time to quibble. I went to the phone, started to lift the receiver, then replaced it. A call might only serve to put someone on his guard. "The phone company should have a cross directory that will give us the address that corresponds with this number. Why don't I give the number to Dockard and let him check it through them?"

"The police overlooked the number," Carlon said. "I see no reason to give it to them now."

I stood, dumbfounded, and stared at him. "You want your daughter found, don't you?"

"Of course! That's why I hired you. But perhaps we should take the incompetence of the Layton police as a measure of luck. As far as I'm concerned, Mr. Nudger, the police are involved in this case only because I have no choice."

I stood in the stale air of the living room, waiting for him to continue. The rattling air conditioner had made little headway, and a bead of perspiration sought its way like a drop of cold mercury down the contours of my ribs.

"What I don't want," Carlon said, "is for the police to be delving into my daughter's private life. There's more at stake here than just the solution to a murder, to which Joan happens to be merely coincidental. Ruthless as it may sound to you, I have my career to consider. And beyond that, certain political possibilities that might surprise you."

"And your daughter's behavior reflects on you, is that it?"

"Not only that. For her own sake I don't want Joan's reputation blackened by aspersions."

"Or facts?"

"Or facts, damn it!"

"We're not only talking about poor judgment here, Mr. Carlon. Withholding evidence in a murder case is illegal. Even a hint of it and I can have my investigator's license revoked and lose my livelihood."

"You'd have me behind you, Nudger. And how long would it take you to earn fifty thousand dollars?"

I put my fists on my hips, started to pace on the red shag. I didn't like what he was suggesting, not only because it was illegal but because it was dangerous. I'd counted on the police involvement to give me at least some protection if and when I crossed paths with Branly's killer, and there was a factor in this case that made that crossing of paths even more likely than Carlon thought. I wondered if he'd considered that the death trap that had killed Branly might have been meant for Joan Clark. After all, it was her car, and going to the Laundromat was still basically a woman's chore.

"I'm not suggesting that we automatically withhold from the police everything you turn up," Carlon said with a note of exasperation. "Whenever you learn something of importance, we can determine whether the police should share in the information. Remember—you're searching for Joan, they're searching for Branly's murderer."

"What about this phone number?"

Carlon smiled. "I'll have it checked for an address, confidentially. I'll phone you later today w ch the information." He walked over, rested his m on my shoulder in a grand gesture of camarader . "After all, it might not be anything important. Thi night be the phone number of a dry cleaner or delic ssen. . . ."

"Or Laundromat."

The smile stayed but the arm went. "That might be, Mr. Nudger. We'll just have to determine the facts."

We left 355 Star Lane together. I sat in my car for a minute, fixing into my key case the house key Carlon had given me. As I looked up, I saw Carlon lift a manicured hand from his steering wheel in a parting wave as he passed me in his Mercedes. He'd bought a lot for his fifty thousand. That "let the buyer beware" adage is backward.

But Carlon was good for his word on the phone number. He called me that afternoon at the Clover Inn and gave me a name and address on Dade Avenue, and he asked me to phone him as soon as I'd checked it out.

Daisy Rogers was the name. I was hoping the number wouldn't belong to a woman. What if Branly had been seeing Daisy Rogers on the sly? That would explain the concealed phone number, and whatever information it might lead to about Branly would be just what he'd chosen to let her know about himself. Probably very little.

I got directions to Dade Avenue from Eddie at the motel office and found that the street was only three blocks east of the motel, though the 2200 address I wanted was some distance south.

The 2200 block of Dade turned out to be a palm-lined street of inexpensive stucco houses set almost at the curb, as if the wide avenue had eroded the front lawns like the sea. The address Carlon had given me was on the corner, a small house painted a pale flamingo pink. A screened-in porch ran across the front of the house, and in the front yard was an old wheelbarrow, also painted pink, used as a planter and exploding with a colorful display of flowers. When I got near the porch, I saw that the screening was old and rusty, paint peeling about the framework.

After five rings of the bell the door was opened by a very old woman with lank gray hair hanging down onto her forehead. She was thin to the point of being emaciated, and age had bent her and humped her narrow back.

I caught myself staring at her. "Daisy Rogers?"

"That's me," she said brightly.

"The Branlys wanted me to let you know they'd be out of town for a few days." I knew I'd be safe in telling her that, since Carlon had kept David Branly's death out of the Layton papers.

She peered at me with lusterless eyes and cocked her head. "The who?"

"The Branlys—David Branly. He gave me your address and phone number. I was going to call you but was near here anyway on business, so I thought I'd relay the message personally."

Daisy Rogers shook her head slowly. She might have been seventy or ninety. "Don't know any Branlys."

63

I endeavored to look as puzzled as I felt. "Are you sure? . . . This is your address and phone number, isn't it?" I handed her a piece of paper with the information.

She placed an ancient pair of rimless spectacles, somebody's future heirloom, on the bridge of her nose, moved out closer to the sunlight and concentrated on the paper for almost a full minute. A musty scent wafted out of the house behind her. "Yep. You're at the right place. Maybe these Branlys know my boy Mark."

"Is he home?"

"Should be soon. Why don't you come in? Or you can sit there and wait on the shady end of the porch if you want. Cooler than inside."

I'd decided to wait on the wooden glider suspended on rusty chains from the porch ceiling when Daisy Rogers looked past me and white eyebrows raised on her speckled forehead.

"There's Mark now."

I turned to see a tall, stooped man, bald with a fringe of gray, shuffling toward the porch steps. He was carrying a paper bag, and he looked, if anything, older than his mother.

"Mark, this is Mister. . . ."

"I came with a message from the Branlys," I told him.

"Damn young punk bastards!" he said, wobbling his head as if he hadn't heard.

"The Branlys?" I asked.

"All of 'em! I don't mind their fashions and their alley cat morals, but I don't like to be cheated without 'em botherin' to try to fool me!"

I stood patiently and let him talk, knowing I hadn't made contact.

"Took this new shirt back"—he held up the wrinkled bag—"'cause it ripped under the arms when I put it on. Young clerk said he couldn't take it back 'cause it was torn. Told him that was why I brung it back! He said he knew the material was weak; that's why the shirt was on sale. Turned his back on me!"

"Keep yourself calm, Mark," his mother put in.

"Did you ever!" he said.

"I ever," I told him. "Do you know Branly?"

He stared at me as if I'd dropped from the porch ceiling. "Don't know any Branlys, didn't I tell you?"

"No, sir."

"Offer you a cold beer?"

I declined with thanks.

As I left, he was trying clumsily to light a pipe while discoursing on the advantages of wooden matches over the new paper ones.

In the sun-heated compact I sat for a minute and looked around at the other houses. I had come to the address Carlon had given me, and Daisy Rogers had confirmed the telephone number. It was possible I'd misread one of the numerals scratched in the woodwork by the Star Lane phone. I started the car and drove farther south on Dade Avenue, until it intersected Palm Road.

The air conditioner Carlon had turned on yesterday was still humming its rattling tune, and the air inside the Star Lane house was almost breathable. I shut the door behind me and went directly to the phone and examined the numbers scratched on the underside of the woodwork. They were as clearly legible as I remembered.

A phone directory rested on the crosspiece of the telephone table's wooden leg braces. I reached down for the directory, opened the front cover, then tossed the book onto the red shag carpet. Picking up the telephone by the hand-hold behind the receiver cradle, I brought it down with me as I settled onto the carpet, next to the directory, and leaned my back against the wall. I opened the directory and began going down the line, dialing long-distance area codes, then the number scratched into the woodwork.

As each distant telephone was answered, I would ask for David Branly, then Vic Branly, and I would try to gauge the reaction of whoever was on the other end of the line. What I most often got was a vague puzzlement, sometimes annoyance.

I was beginning to perspire, and my back was aching from leaning against the hardness of the wall. Then finally, after dialing area code 312 and the phone number that was now etched in my memory as deeply as it was in the woodwork, I got the sort of reaction I'd been seeking.

"Dave? . . ." came the puzzled voice after I'd spoken. "There is no David Branly here . . ." It was a man's voice, nasal and uncertain.

"What about Vic?" I asked.

"Who is this?"

"A friend of Dave's."

A click and a buzz greeted that statement.

I replaced the receiver in its cradle and waited, watching a fly crawl laboriously up the opposite wall. As if the altitude had become too much for it, the fly began to veer to the right as it neared the ceiling. Something was making a hissing sound in the quiet room—my breathing.

The telephone rang.

On the third ring I picked up the receiver and pressed it to my ear, said nothing.

"Hello, Dave? . . ." came the same voice that had been on the line a few minutes before. "Vic? . . ."

Gently I replaced the receiver, picked it up again for a dial tone. Dale Carlon's secretary followed her instructions and rushed through my call to him.

"How long would it take you to get me a name and address for the Daisy Rogers number with a 312 area code?" I asked Carlon. "Probably in Chicago."

66

"You mean it's not a local number?"

"Not for our purposes. A very old woman and her son live at the Dade address."

"What about the son?"

"He seems older than the mother and has rips in his shirt."

There was little time in Carlon's day for digression. His telephone voice was terse. "I should be able to have that corresponding name and address for you within an hour."

"I'll be waiting at the Star Lane phone," I told him and got off the line so he could get busy.

Sitting on the carpet with my arms crossed on my knees, I wondered if Carlon could do it, if his influence carried that far from Layton.

I got up, stretched, and walked around the cramped, oppressive living room to work the stiffness from my aging bones. The air seemed to get staler, the walls closer together.

An hour and ten minutes had passed when Carlon called back.

The phone number belonged to a man named Roger Horvell, 67 Sirilla Street, in Chicago. I thanked Carlon, then punched and freed the cradle button to get a dial tone. After talking to Eastern Airlines in Orlando, I drove to the Clover Inn to pack.

This time Lieutenant Dockard was waiting for me.

9

Dockard was standing with his foot propped on the dusty front bumper of his unmarked car, parked in front of my cabin. He smiled as I parked next to him, looking over my rented compact as if pondering whether to get one for himself.

I got out of the car, nodded to him and walked over to where he was standing.

"You and I need to talk," Dockard told me, squinting into the sun behind me but holding his friendly smile.

"We talked a lot yesterday," I said.

Dockard didn't move from his relaxed position, but I could see he was waiting for me to invite him inside, out of the heat. I decided to let the sun work for me and keep the conversation short.

"We need to understand a few things about your working for Dale Carlon," Dockard said, seeing that our talk was going to be brief and getting to the point. "Mr. Carlon has . . . let's say a habit of stepping outside the rules sometimes and doing things in his own fashion."

"You were careful to explain that to me yesterday."

Dockard picked at an imaginary wart on his palm. "I understand the confidence you owe Mr. Carlon," he said, weighing each word for its potential to boomerang, "but you also have some responsibility to the law. Mr. Carlon means well, but he's not a professional like we are. He might get some mistaken notions. . . ."

"Any particular notion in mind?" I asked.

A large mosquito droned in unpredictable circles around Dockard's head, sizing him up. Dockard swatted the air where the mosquito had been. "What I mean, Nudger, is that the more people we have working on this case, the sooner it's likely to be solved. I wouldn't want you to think it would be best to withhold anything from the Layton police. And of course we'll share whatever we know with you."

There was a something-for-nothing offer. Dockard wouldn't dare withhold anything pertinent from me now that I represented Dale Carlon.

"I'm aware of my obligation to the law," I said.

"I'm sure. It's just that Mr. Carlon, well-meaning as he is, might instruct you to operate, sometimes, with us still in the dark. And I think, considering the circumstances of the case, that I owe you a certain confidence if you keep me informed."

"Without Carlon's knowledge?"

"I'm only asking you to obey the law, Nudger." He flicked a hand again at the phantom mosquito.

What Dockard was saying was that whenever Carlon instructed me to keep something from the Layton police, I could tell Dockard without fear of Carlon's finding out. It was less serious to betray a client's trust than to withhold evidence in a murder investigation, and Dockard was giving me the opportunity to exchange one transgression for the other. I remembered his words of yesterday, about Carlon being the one man not to cross; and today he was asking me to do just that.

"You're telling me I can have it both ways," I said.

"If that's how you want to think of it. Either way I'd like you to keep this talk confidential."

"You've got that."

"At least my way, if Mr. Carlon does have some wrong suggestions, you've got an out."

At the risk of fifty thousand dollars, I thought, not to mention the possibility of Carlon's revenge. I doubted if Dockard knew the stakes were that high. People like Carlon confused things.

"If the situation comes up," I said to Dockard, "I'll think about it."

There was something in his face that made me feel he knew the situation already had come up. He nodded, removed his foot from the dusty chrome bumper. "It's something for you to consider."

Now the mosquito began droning about me. I'd thought it was my friend. Dockard walked around to the driver's side of the car and opened the door.

"I remember Joan Clark," he said before he got in. "She's not going to be found easily if she doesn't want to be."

I stood and watched Dockard drive off the lot. He yielded to an overloaded station wagon making a left to get to the Clover Inn's office, then his plain car, with its square-tipped shortwave antenna, merged with the light traffic on Main Drive.

Dockard had given me something to think about. Was his proposition made out of a genuine concern to solve Branly's murder and find Joan Clark as soon as possible? Or was he trying to make sure that the Layton police department and Lieutenant Dockard accomplished whatever was needed and received full credit from Carlon? I didn't doubt that the latter might be his motive. A man like Carlon could do a lot for a police lieutenant like Dockard in a town like Layton.

I swatted at the mosquito.

There was another very strong possibility I couldn't overlook. Was Carlon aware of Dockard's visit? After our conversation at the Star Lane house, had he asked the lieutenant to put the proposition to me to test me?

That possibility was reason fifty thousand and one for me to play the game straight with Carlon and to not mention to Lieutenant Dockard that I was going to Chicago.

10

My flight arrived at Chicago's O'Hare International on time to the minute. After making my way through the crowd that was bustling to the incomprehensible rhythm of the public address speakers, I claimed my luggage and took a Continental limo into the city.

At one of the big hotels on North Michigan, I got out and left my luggage in the check room. There was no point in registering anywhere yet; I had no way of knowing if my stay in Chicago would last for days or for hours. Outside the hotel I got into one of the cabs parked in single waiting line at the curb and gave the driver Roger Horvell's address.

After a drive through the hippiness-mellowing-to-campiness of Old Town, the taxi entered an area of recent renovation and pulled to the curb in front of a fairly new tall building with a glassed-in lobby that gave off a silvery mirrored effect. I paid the driver, left the cab, then watched my image ascend the concrete steps and reach for the push plate on one of the wide glass double doors.

The lobby featured a small, bubbling Florentine fountain that on close inspection appeared to be constructed entirely of plastic. I walked around the fountain and crossed the scuffed tile floor to a bank of metal mailboxes by an ornate wrought iron gate that blocked access to the elevators. I pressed the pearled plastic button beneath Horvell's mail slot.

He was home. I identified myself over the intercom and told him I wanted to see him regarding David Branly. His nasal voice betrayed confusion and maybe a little fright as he invited me to come up. I understood how he felt; my own gut was beginning to tighten with

71

apprehension. A buzzer sounded, and I passed through the wrought iron gateway and rode the elevator to the fifth floor.

Roger Horvell was a small man in his late twenties, balding prematurely, with thick glasses and a large nose a bit too bulbous to be charitably called hawklike. He was wearing window-check pants and a loose-fitting brown knit pullover shirt with an alligator sewn above the pocket. His casual attire didn't fit his nervousness.

"What is it about David?" he asked, pacing to a large window that afforded a view of the building across the street. It was a taller building than the one we were in, with draped and private windows.

Horvell's nervousness made me feel more confident. I sat on a modern, uncomfortable and obviously inexpensive sofa, noticing that the plush blue carpeting in the new apartment was already beginning to wear. "I need some information about Branly," I said, "and unfortunately he's in no position to help me."

Horvell turned to face me, scratched a scrawny arm as if he had poison ivy. "Is Dave in some kind of trouble?"

"It could be put that way," I said.

He nodded jerkily, sighed, as if he'd expected to hear that news. "You said you were a private detective. What has that to do with David?"

"Nothing directly. Where do you know Branly from?"

Horvell hesitated, then the apprehensive, magnified eyes behind the thick lenses seemed to register the expression of a man waist deep in cold water who has decided to submerge the rest of himself. "We worked together, for the same company."

"What company?"

"David hasn't done anything, has he?"

"No," I said, and waited silently for the answer to my question.

Horvell ran a hand over his balding head as if he still had a mop of hair. "High Grade Hardware," he said in a resigned, nasal tone. "I still work there."

"How long has Branly been gone?"

"Almost a year."

"Fired or quit?"

"Neither," Horvell said hastily. "He was a good company man, one of the best at High Grade, but his job of secondary cost analyst became obsolete."

"If he was so competent, why didn't the company keep him and work him into some other job?" I asked, wondering just what a secondary cost analyst was.

Horvell smiled bitterly. "Things are tight at High Grade, as they are now in most businesses. But blood is still thick, and as in most businesses, there's a certain amount of nepotism at High Grade. David's job was primarily a backup position in a system of double checks that the company felt they could eliminate. I know for sure they didn't want to let him go, but a favored nephew was 'working his way up' in the organization, and since David had no marketing experience. . . ."

"How long had Branly worked there?"

"About five years—the same as me. We were brought here to the main office at the same time, got to be good friends. I frankly admired him for his shrewdness and ambition."

I sat there with the feeling that all this information wouldn't get me anywhere, or Horvell wouldn't be giving it to me.

"Where did Branly go after he left High Grade?" I asked.

Horvell's mouth opened and closed and he shrugged his thin shoulders.

"I have certain restrictions on what I can tell you without my client's consent, Mr. Horvell, but I *can* tell you that you're not helping Branly anymore by keeping his secrets."

"You called here this morning, didn't you?"

I nodded.

He peeled off his glasses, wiped them on his shirt and looked at me myopically. "Who is your client, Mr. Nudger?"

I had a good idea of what button to press to get Horvell's cooperation. "Have you heard of Carlon Plastics?"

"Of course."

"My client is Dale Carlon, president and chairman of the board."

"Christ!"

"Almost."

Horvell paced back and looked out the wide window. That seemed to be a favorite move of his to gather his thoughts. I saw his shoulders square, and he turned to face me again and replaced his glasses on his oversize nose.

"You're investigating something criminal?"

"Yes, and I advise you strongly not to implicate yourself by lying to me. I understand your loyalty, Mr. Horvell, and I do give you my word that nothing you tell me can be used to harm Branly."

"He lived here for a while," Horvell said, "after he was let go at High Grade. It was a matter of economics. The company wasn't able to give him much severance pay. I was glad to help him."

"How long did he live here?"

"Until about three months ago. Then he got some money from somewhere, moved into an apartment with a girl he was going with."

"An apartment where?"

"He never would tell me, and that's the truth."

"Did you ever meet the girl?"

Horvell nodded. "A few times. Joan Clark was her name."

"This her?" I showed him one of the photographs Gordon Clark had given me.

"Yes, that's the same girl," Horvell said. There was something else he wanted to say. I waited patiently for him to get it out. "You'll be doing more checking, won't you? Asking questions at High Grade Hardware?"

"I plan to."

"Then there's . . . something else," Horvell admitted. "David Branly never worked there. There is no David Branly. His real name is Victor Talbert."

"Why did he change it?"

"He never said. He changed it after he moved out. I asked him once but he was evasive." Horvell stuttered a nervous, nasal laugh. "I really don't know much; that's why I don't so much mind trying to answer your questions."

I believed him there. He saw that he'd been drawn into something with the potential to pull him all the way under. I was in a perfect position to sympathize.

"What other friends of Victor Talbert's did you meet?" I asked.

"None," Horvell said quickly. "The only friends we really had in common were from the office, and Vic seemed to lose interest in them entirely after he was let go. He formed new friendships somewhere. I don't know what he did while I was working; one reason we shared the apartment was because of my long working hours. We knew we'd seldom get in each other's way."

"You remember him or this Joan Clark mentioning any names?"

Horvell bit his lower lip and thought hard. I expected him to pace to the window, but he didn't. "One," he said finally. "Somebody or something named Congram. I remember because Vic mentioned the name once and Joan seemed to get angry."

"That's all—Congram?"

"That's all he said. I don't even remember in what context."

"All the time he was living with you, was Talbert trying to land another job?"

The stuttering laugh came again. "At first he was. Executives like Vic can't, or won't, take just any job. And as scarce as middle management positions are, his back was to the wall. Oh, he had some menial jobs offered to him, but it isn't in Vic's nature to take a step backward."

"How did you come to have Talbert's phone number, Mr. Horvell?"

"About a month ago Vic dropped by here. He said he was going away—wouldn't say where. But he left me his number for a sort of touchstone. He told me he was going to live under the name of David Branly, and he might phone me if he needed anyone, in case of trouble."

"What kind of trouble?"

"I tried to get him to tell me, but he wouldn't. He was frightened, though. I could tell that. It was the first time I'd ever seen him scared. Vic Talbert is the sort of man who exudes confidence."

"What about the girl?" I asked in a throwaway voice.

"Vic said Joan Clark would be with him. And he mentioned something about her little girl."

"Have you talked to him since then?"

"No. When I asked him what I was supposed to do if he phoned, he said 'maybe nothing,' that he'd let me know if the time came."

Horvell walked over to a small portable bar set up in a corner.

"Can I get you something?" he asked.

I told him no thanks and watched him pour himself two fingers of good Scotch. His hands trembled slightly, and the neck of the bottle clinked on the glass and seemed to embarrass him. He knocked down half the drink in one loud gulp. I couldn't be sure that he was uncomfortable because he was hiding something; he was a human nerve.

"I'd like to ask a favor of you, Nudger," he said in an unsteady nasal whine. "When you go to High Grade Hardware, try to leave my name out of it. I just can't afford to be messed up in my career."

"I don't know if that will be possible, Mr. Horvell. Victor Talbert is dead."

I thought he was actually going to drop the glass. It slipped an abrupt inch in his hand, and he staggered to a chair and sat down. "Dead? . . . How did it happen? Was it the trouble Vic talked about? . . ."

"Maybe. He was murdered, Mr. Horvell."

"Murdered! Christ! Is that what you're investigating?"

"No, the police are investigating that, and when they get around to you, I advise you to tell them what you told me. Unless you have something to add."

He shook his head absently. "Murdered . . ." he said unbelievingly to himself.

I thanked him for talking to me and stood to leave. Instead of showing me out he continued sitting and tossed down the rest of his drink. His myopic eyes were desperate. I could almost see his agitated brain writhing like a mass of worms.

"Nudger!" The imploring nasal voice stopped me when my hand touched the doorknob.

I turned and waited for Horvell to wring out whatever he had to say. His mouth worked before any sound came out, as if the air in the apartment had suddenly become too thin to carry sound.

"Do you promise to leave my name out of it, if possible, at High Grade?"

"If possible," I told him.

He stared hard at me and seemed to find me trustworthy, but then, he wanted to so badly.

"Vic was seeing another woman at the same time as Joan Clark," he said, as if we'd struck a deal. "Her name was Belle Dee."

"Do you know where I can find her?"

"I have her address. Vic had me pick him up there one evening." He got up and walked to a small desk near the entrance to the dining room. With a bit of rummaging about in one of the drawers, he found what he was looking for, copied it on another piece of paper and handed it to me.

"Remember about leaving me out of it," he said.

"I'll do what I can," I told him, opening the door.

"Vic, dead . . ." he murmured again unbelievingly, running his hand through his imaginary hair.

"Dead . . . dead . . . dead . . ." I repeated to myself, walking down the long carpeted hall to the elevator, as if that would help to exorcise the growing, twisting sensation of fear in my chest and stomach.

It didn't help.

11

After leaving Horvell's apartment I took a cab to claim my luggage. Then I rented a car—knowing I'd be in town for a while—this time a full-size sedan.

I checked in at the TraveLodge Motel, on South Michigan Avenue, not too far from the headquarters of High Grade Hardware. I made a few phone calls, had dinner and a few drinks to untie my knots, and slept almost as deeply as Victor Talbert.

High Grade Hardware's corporate headquarters turned out to be a tall, square building of what looked to be burnished copper glinting in the bright morning sun. Outside the imposing entrance was a tall aluminum flagpole, and beneath the American flag flew the company's smaller flag, a black crossed hammer and wrench insignia on a field of white.

The reception area inside the entrance was also done up in black and white. I walked over to an astoundingly beautiful blonde seated behind a wide, bare desk and told her who I was and that I had an appointment with T. J. Harper, the personnel manager.

Harper saw me immediately, which surprised the blonde. She didn't know that after a Dale Carlon phone call the president of High Grade Hardware had passed down the word to cooperate with me. I was beginning to experience occasional exhilarating delusions of power, but I knew that I'd still bleed.

T. J. Harper's office continued the black and white motif, with a large plaque with High Grade's hammer and wrench insignia mounted on the wall behind his desk. An affable-looking man with an air of efficiency, Harper was wearing a blue pinstriped suit and a semimilitary haircut that was gray wire at the temples. He smiled a nice smile and motioned for me to sit down, then sat down himself and laced his fingers on his desk top. I felt somewhat like a job applicant.

I told him I appreciated his taking the time to see me and that I wanted information about a former employee at High Grade. He didn't seem surprised when I told him the name of that former employee.

"Victor Talbert was a fine young man," he said, "an ideal employee. It was regrettable that we no longer had a niche in which to fit him. Under present conditions it simply doesn't pay to do some of the things you'd like to do."

"Did Talbert get along all right with the other employees?"

"Certainly," Harper said, as if I'd been indelicate to ask. "He had no enemies here except within the framework of honest competition. If it were possible for Victor Talbert to walk in here today, and an opening suited his qualifications, I'd rehire him without a qualm. He was strictly the victim of declining sales, and job training that became obsolete practically overnight. That sort of thing happens frequently."

"How did he take his dismissal?"

Harper unlaced his fingers and dropped his hands out of sight beneath the desk. There were faint damp spots on the polished wood where his hands had rested. "He was disappointed," Harper said, "but I explained the situation and he understood. At least he said he did."

"Did he mention what he planned to do when he left High Grade? Or have any of his prospective employers contacted you for a reference?"

Harper stood and walked to a file cabinet. He pulled open a long drawer and withdrew a thick file folder as if he'd known exactly where to reach. Seated back at his desk, he flipped the folder open and leafed through the contents.

"It's a fine record," he said. "High scores on every sort of test, several commendations from superiors. Here's what I want—yes, a bank, First Security Trust, called on the thirteenth of last month in regard to a loan application Victor Talbert had submitted to them. They learned nothing here that would discourage them from granting him the loan."

"Loan for what?"

"That I couldn't tell you. Banks don't go into detail on such matters." Teeth flashed in a confidential smile. "Usually we here at High Grade don't reveal anything we might consider personal about present or past employees. If it weren't for the extenuating circumstances in Victor's case, you wouldn't have gotten in to see me."

I'd been put in my place. Outside Harper's window I could see the corner of the white company flag cracking in the breeze.

"Of course, you found that out earlier," Harper said, still smiling.

The office was suddenly cold. "Earlier?"

Now the smile faded. "Yes, didn't you phone yesterday morning for an appointment?"

"This appointment was arranged for me."

"But I thought. . . . Well, someone called here yesterday and requested to see me regarding Victor Talbert. The caller was informed that High Grade Hardware has a policy that forbids giving out any unauthorized personnel information."

"Did the caller leave a name?"

"No, that's why I thought you'd called." The intercom buzzed and a female voice informed Harper that someone named Mr. Sathers wanted to see him at his earliest convenience. That seemed to put Harper on edge. "Mr. Sathers is the top man," he explained.

I took my cue to get to the essentials. "Mr. Harper, did you know anything about Victor Talbert's social life, what he did after hours?"

He drummed his fingertips, thinking. "No . . . not really. He attended all the company functions, handled himself quite well. He was well mannered, didn't drink to excess and possessed an admirable sense of tact. I'd be very surprised if there was anything . . . irregular about Victor."

"He was earmarked for bigger things here, wasn't he, until the presence of a favorite nephew eased him out?"

Harper's expression didn't change but his color darkened and a vein throbbed briefly at his graying temple. "I don't know who you've been talking to," he said, "but that's hardly an accurate way of describing the situation. Sheer economics dictated that someone had to go. Victor's job specialty was no longer needed, and to utilize his talents anywhere else would have meant a costly retraining and breaking-in period."

"And the nephew had this training?"

"Precisely." He leaned back, laced his fingers again. "Mr. Nudger, at Victor Talbert's level, potential isn't enough."

I nodded. Harper couldn't tell me flatly that Talbert had potentially been the superior of the two employees.

"Not that it matters now," he said.

"It might matter," I told him, "only not to Victor Talbert."

"I understand he's been murdered. Any ideas as to who and why?"

Carlon must have had to divulge the fact of Talbert's murder to get my appointment with Harper. "None here," I said. "That's more in the police department's line."

Harper shifted in his chair and licked his lips. I could see he wanted to say more but knew he shouldn't.

"Do you have any past or present employees named Congram?" I asked.

Harper pressed his intercom button and repeated my question to his secretary in the outer office.

Within a minute she buzzed him back with a negative answer.

It had been a blind stab anyway. "What's the nephew's name?" I asked.

"Paul Madden."

"Is he in the building now?"

"Probably."

"I'd like to talk to him. And I'd like to talk to whoever was Victor Talbert's direct supervisor."

"They're busy," Harper said, "but I'll arrange it." He punched a button on his desk phone for an inside line and cleared the way for me. I thanked him, shook hands with him and left his black and white office.

After getting myself lost several times in the building's labyrinth of halls, I managed to talk to both Madden and Victor Talbert's old supervisor, a tall, stern man named Graham Winkler. Madden had seemed a decent, sympathetic sort, somehow too lethargic for his surroundings. He told me he'd felt bad about Talbert's dismissal but that Talbert had taken it well and they'd remained friends, even to the point of having an after work drink together on Talbert's last day at High Grade.

Winkler substantiated what both Harper and Madden had told me. Victor Talbert had been highly thought of, considered an ideal company man. He was keenly intelligent, remarkably ambitious, and above all, a realist. I thought I detected a touch of resentment in Winkler over Talbert's dismissal, and I didn't blame him, if the man had been such a whiz. He'd have made any supervisor look good.

Talbert's past, as I uncovered it, wasn't exactly shaping him up to be the fugitive murder victim he'd become. Ambitious, hard working, a young man who inspired admiration and loyalty, he'd been the type a father would want his daughter to marry, the type Dale Carlon might have chosen for his own daughter Joan. Then had come the break in the pattern—the fear Horvell had described—and the blast of a rigged shotgun in a parked car in Florida. I needed to know the reason and was almost afraid to discover it.

The things a man will do for money. . . . You think the temptation doesn't apply to you, that you're too solid and sensible to bend, until the time arrives and temptation becomes opportunity.

One thing I knew was that I didn't belong in a place like this, with its contrived pressures, strict written and unwritten rules that had to be obeyed if you wanted to survive, much less advance, in the pecking order. That advancement was the important thing, the thing that drove the Talberts of the world.

I found my way out of High Grade's headquarters,

passing in the hall several dignified-looking types with gold hammer-and-wrench insignia pins on their lapels. As I walked toward my car, I could hear the snap of the flags and the dull metallic thumping of rope against the tall aluminum flagpole. I wondered idly if High Grade employees held a ceremony each morning as they raised the flags, and I wondered which flag they saluted.

Before starting the car I reached into my shirt pocket and pulled out the slip of paper that Horvell had given me with Belle Dee's address written on it. I laid the paper beside me on the front seat and unfolded a Chicago and surrounding area street map. Without much difficulty I located the street I wanted and used a ballpoint pen to circle it.

12

I drove from High Grade headquarters directly to Belle Dee's address.

She lived in one of a line of old four-story brick apartment buildings on Lampan Street, in a neighborhood in the gray area of urban decay. Several small businesses were hanging on in the block—a men's clothing store, a jeweler, a secondhand shop, and on the corner a little Italian restaurant with an unappetizing, mottled red sign that was supposed to represent a pizza. There were a few clusters of the young and denim-clad on the sidewalks and an old couple walking a big, fine German shepherd.

Belle Dee lived on the third floor, up steep and newly painted creaking stairs. The still-drying paint overpowered some of the normal apartment scents of cooking, and lingering disinfectant. I found the door with Belle Dee's number on it and knocked, experiencing my "nobody home" feeling.

No answer.

When I knocked again, louder, the door across the hall opened and a stocky man with a bushy head of hair and a large brown mustache looked out at me. Aside from the fact that he was barefoot, he was fully dressed in tan slacks and a silky shirt with swirling orange designs all over it.

"You looking for Belle Dee?" he asked, smiling.

I told him I was.

The smile got wider. He was justifiably proud of his teeth. "You're not a process server or anything, are you?"

"No, I was told to look her up by a mutual friend." I let him make what he wanted of that. He decided he wanted to believe me.

"She's probably working at the Poptop Club," he said, stroking his brown mustache, "about four blocks east on Delorel. Easy to find."

He was right about the Poptop Club's being easy to find. It dominated the block of seedy buildings with a tall sign that proclaimed it to be the home of "the biggest and the best."

There was no sign of either of those as I entered and looked around. I was in a long room, bar to the right, tables and chairs to the left and booths along one wall. At the end opposite the door was a raised stage with a purple-curtained backdrop and some speakers aimed out over the tables so that no one could escape the sound. There was another platform, about eight feet off the floor, behind the bar and supported from the raised ceiling by heavy silver-colored chains.

The Poptop must not have had much day trade. It was peopled only by a bearded, purple-shirted bartender and two customers morosely sipping beer in one of the booths. I walked to the bar and ordered a bourbon and water, which I needed.

"I was told I could find Belle Dee here," I said to the bartender when he set my drink on its coaster.

"You can, but it'll have to be after five."

"She wait tables here?"

"That and dances," the bartender said. "All the girls here double up."

"I checked her apartment. Any idea where I can find her now? It's important to her."

"She might be at the beach. Spends a lot of warm days there."

"Which part of the beach?"

"Why? You going to look for her?"

"Probably." I sipped my drink, which was on the weak side.

"Wish I was going with you," he said.

While I finished my drink, he described Belle Dee as a tall, blue-eyed blonde with dark eyebrows and long hair, and he gave me easily understood if overstated directions to her favorite strip of beach.

"You can't miss her," he said, as I got down off my bar stool to leave. "She's got . . . you know." He cupped both hands about six inches from his chest. "Outstanding!" he added.

I nodded knowingly.

It was a warm day and there were a lot of outstanding "you knows" at the beach. I stood for a while and watched but could not determine which belonged to Belle Dee.

I gave up trying to figure it out, bought myself a hamburger and Coke for lunch and sat watching a young boy trying vainly to bury his overweight father in the sand. The boy was about the age my own son would be. I pushed away the maudlin mood that threatened to envelope me, leaned back and watched wisps of white cloud over the sparkling lake water.

The breeze off the lake was a soothing massage, and the shouts and laughter of the bathers were pleasantly muted by vastness. I could understand why Belle Dee liked it here. I stayed longer than I should have.

It cost me a two-dollar cover charge when I returned to the Poptop Club that evening. The personality of the club seemed to have changed with the setting sun. Now it was crowded, the only light coming from candles on each table and flickering purple flashes of brilliance in time to the frenzied music bursting from the band on the rear stage. Dancers writhed about the small, crowded dance floor between tables and bar, and several fantastically built waitresses in skimpy but unimaginative costumes wove among the tables with trays of drinks. I took a table near the booths, and one of the waitresses appeared immediately to take my order.

When she returned with my bourbon and water I told her I wanted to talk to Belle Dee, repeating it several times so she could read my lips.

"You'll have to wait!" she shouted through the din. ". . . dances next!" She pointed toward the suspended platform behind the bar.

I sipped my weak drink and waited, and within a few minutes there was a blast of music, the suspended platform was spotlighted and Belle Dee danced.

She was tall, and her long blonde hair swaying in rhythm to the music made her seem more graceful than she was. Her spectacular, gyrating body was probably the siliconed product of science, and the amazing thing was that she managed to keep everything from going in the same direction at once, maybe for fear the building would shift.

She finished her dance to loud, enthusiastic applause punctuated by shouts, whistles and a few remarks she pretended not to hear. Ten minutes later she appeared at my table in street clothes, a surprisingly plain blue dress with a sash belt and flat shoes. "I don't know you," she said.

"You know Victor Talbert. I'd like to talk to you about him." I waved a hand for her to sit down.

"Police?"

"No." I caught the attention of a waitress and bought Belle Dee a drink—one I'd never seen before, tall and tropical and made with gin. "My name's Alo Nudger," I said. "I'm a private detective, and I promise that nothing you tell me will be used to harm Victor."

"He's not married, is he?"

"No. He's involved indirectly in what I'm working on. How long's it been since you've seen him?"

She trained almond-shaped blue eyes on me as if she'd just noticed me across the table; there was an emptiness in them; they were doll's eyes. I didn't think she was going to answer, but she did. "It's been . . . three, four months, maybe."

"You were seriously involved with him, weren't you?"

"We had it going between us, but we weren't serious."

I thought about asking her what the hell that meant, but decided against it. She must have seen the puzzlement in my eyes.

"Vic wasn't serious about me," she said, "and he knew I wasn't about him. I was interested in fun and he was interested in what interests all men."

I nodded. "An honest arrangement. Did Talbert have any enemies you can remember?"

She laughed—a musical laugh, but it was the blues. "Vic was too much of a square head to have any enemies. He played life right out of the rule book, an up-standing, ambitious citizen. If you cut him he'd bleed apple pie."

"Then he wasn't into drugs, that sort of thing?"

"Too straight for that, straight but nice. He didn't even drink heavy."

"How'd you meet him?"

"Oh, something like the way I met you. He came in here one night, wanted to talk to me. Next night he was back. I liked him, but I saw he was gonna get hurt. He was too afraid of failing at anything—he wanted to be a success so bad it burned. The hell with that kind of stuff."

I smiled at her. "He doesn't sound like your type."

When she smiled back I could understand what Talbert had seen in her. She had that bony symmetry beneath velvet skin that inspires casting directors. "Don't get the idea Vic doesn't know how to have a good time," she said. "I think he has to cut loose now and then, uptight as he is."

"Did he come in here often?"

"Quite a bit. But not in the last few months."

"Didn't you wonder where he was?"

"I didn't care. That was our arrangement."

I felt almost a cruel desire to shock her, to instill some feeling into her beauty. "Talbert is dead. He was murdered."

Immediately I regretted the bluntness of my words, but I honestly didn't know if I'd reached her or not. She lowered her head so I couldn't see her eyes, and a tightness crept into her features. Then she raised her head and looked directly at me. "No kidding!"

"Any idea who killed him?" I asked.

"None. He must have been mistaken for somebody else."

I ordered us each another drink. "Did you know any of his friends?"

She shook her head no. "It was just me and Vic."

"Did he ever mention Joan Clark?"

"Not that I can recall."

"What about the name Congram?"

Something like recognition came into her eyes. "That's right, yeah. Vic knew somebody named Congram; really thought he was important, from what I gathered. But he only mentioned the name a few times. I didn't pry." She drained half of her fresh drink. "Dead, huh?" I wasn't sure, but I thought her eyes glistened with more than their usual moisture. Or the light might have done her a favor.

The band, which had been taking a break since Belle Dee's dance, blasted out with another discordant specialty.

"They're lousy," Belle Dee said, "but lousy with a beat. Listen, I've got some of Vic's stuff at my apartment. What am I gonna do with it?"

I swirled the ice in my glass to appear disinterested. "What kind of stuff?"

"Clothes, mostly. Just stuff he left there."

"Mind letting me look it over?"

"I don't know if I should."

"I'll bet you do a lot you shouldn't."

She laughed her blues laugh. "You're right; it doesn't make any difference to me. I can let you look at the stuff when I get off at midnight." She finished her drink and stood, attracting eyes. "I gotta get back to work."

I told her I'd see her at twelve.

She smiled and turned toward the crowded dance floor, disappearing in a blast of flashing blue light and drums.

I made my drink last another twenty minutes and left.

The hours remaining before it was time to meet Belle Dee I spent in my motel room, lying on my back in bed and trying to figure out where events were taking me.

How was it going to set with the law when they found out I'd withheld the information that Branly was actually Victor Talbert, that I'd gone through some of his effects? I knew that eventually it would all have to come out; I didn't think even Carlon could keep that from happening. I hoped he could; I hoped I wasn't being cynical enough.

I thought about Belle Dee and then Lornee. The coldness grew in my stomach, and blood pulsed in my ears. I concentrated on the fifty thousand dollars.

At ten thirty I phoned Dale Carlon and filled him in on my activities, and I asked him if he could smooth the way for me to talk to someone at First Security Trust about Talbert's loan application. Carlon told me he'd see what he could do and then call me in the morning.

It was almost twelve thirty when Belle Dee fished a glittering jeweled key ring from her purse and let us into her apartment on Lampan Street.

We were in a small living room, furnished glass-topped and chrome modern. A jaggedly designed tapestry hung on one wall above a long black-vinyl sofa that couldn't have been more than six inches off the floor. Beneath the clear glass top of a coffee table before the sofa was a plastic flower arrangement.

Belle Dee tossed her purse onto a chair and went into the kitchen. She returned in less than a minute with two glasses containing generous measures of bourbon on the rocks and held out one of the drinks for me. I accepted that and her offer to sit on the low black couch.

"Vic's things are in the other room," she said. "I'll be right back."

I sat and watched her walk into what I assumed was

the bedroom. The low sofa was more comfortable than it looked, and there was a pleasant, faintly perfumed quietness about the apartment that was relaxing.

Belle Dee returned carrying some folded clothes, an attaché case and a pair of shiny black wing-tip shoes. "This is all Vic left, Mr . . . Nudger?"

"Call me Alo."

"That sounds foreign."

"Sometimes I think it is."

She handed Talbert's possessions down to me then sat next to me on the sofa while I examined them. I was disappointed to find that the attaché case, a metal-trimmed, expensive model, was empty but for a black knit tie. The clothing promised little more—a wrinkled pair of slacks, neatly folded undershirt and a white windbreaker. The pants pockets were empty, but when I felt inside the jacket pockets my fingers touched a thin, stiff rectangle of cardboard. I withdrew my hand without it, set the folded clothes aside and finished my drink.

"Mind?" I asked, holding out the glass.

Belle Dee checked her own near-empty glass. "I could use a refill myself."

When she'd disappeared into the kitchen, I drew the business card from the jacket pocket and examined it before slipping it into my own pocket. It was a plain white card engraved only with GRATUITY INSURANCE. No address, no phone number. On the back of the card a name was penciled in angled, hasty print: Robert Manners. Another Victor Talbert AKA?

Belle Dee returned with the drinks and sat next to me again on the sofa. "Did anything of Vic's help you?"

"Hard to say. It was worth a look."

"You can take it all with you if you'd like."

"I'd keep it if I were you. Eventually the police might want it."

She made an expression as if she hadn't thought of that and raised her glass to her lips. There was a softness in her eyes, maybe from the bourbon, and I fancied I could feel the heat from the closeness of her lushly perfect body.

"Ever get tired of living alone?" I asked.

"Everybody does sometimes."

I reached out and traced the line of her pale cheek with the backs of my fingers. She drew away, more with the change in her eyes than any motion of her head.

"I'm not lonely tonight," she said, "only sometimes." A smile to show me she regarded the effort as a compliment.

I returned the smile with a futile one of my own and stood.

"Thanks for showing me Talbert's effects," I told her. I let her know where I was staying and asked her to contact me if anything else about Talbert came to mind.

"If you have any more questions," Belle Dee said, "come around to the club."

We both knew the answer to the current question was no, so I said good-night and left.

13

The jangling telephone by my bed yanked me out of sleep at nine the next morning.

It was Carlon, as promised. He told me that arranging for me to get what information I needed from First Security Trust had been difficult, but that he'd managed it. The bank was one of an affiliation of Midwestern banks with which three of the Carlon plants did business. He told me to ask for a man named Tom McGregor, the loan officer who'd processed Talbert's application.

I thanked Carlon and asked him if he'd heard of Gratuity Insurance. He hadn't. And he said the name Robert Manners meant nothing to him.

When Carlon hung up I placed a call to Lieutenant Frank Dockard in Layton. When he answered the phone, he seemed not at all surprised to hear from me. By now he'd know I left Layton. I assumed he knew I was calling from Chicago.

"I'd like you to check on a Robert Manners for me," I told him.

"Who's he?"

"I don't know. That's why I phoned you. Anything new in Layton?"

"The bullets taken from the Star Lane house were thirty-eight caliber, from the same gun, if that helps you any."

"You never can tell."

"Anything I should know, Nudger?"

"I don't think so."

"What number are you calling from? So I can phone and let you know if there's anything on Manners."

"I'll call you, Lieutenant. Sometime this afternoon. And thanks." Before he could reply I hung up.

I dressed, had a quick buckwheat pancake breakfast and headed for First Security Trust. The extent of Carlon's influence amazed me. His nationwide corporation seemed to touch everywhere in the business community. What he could accomplish with his index finger on the telephone was to me the most startling revelation of the case. He'd mentioned political prospects that might surprise me. Maybe that was part of it; maybe it was known that Carlon might soon be in a position to do some important people important favors. I wondered, how many Carlons were there, how many men with that kind of encompassing influence on other lives?

First Security Trust was one of Chicago's older banks. There was more polished wood and marble in the lobby than formica. Half a dozen female tellers were at their windows, and the bank was active with customers either waiting in short lines or standing and writing at long, elbow-high tables.

I identified myself and asked a young girl at the information desk for Mr. McGregor. She spoke for a moment on the phone, and soon after she hung up, McGregor came into the lobby to greet me.

He was a middle-aged man, short and overweight, with a seamed, smiling face and a broken-veined drinker's nose. Not at all the banker type. After a firm handshake he led me behind the tellers' cages to one of a series of small, frosted-glass cubicles, each containing a desk and chair. He moved behind the desk and motioned toward the chair with a smile, waiting for me to be seated before he sat down. I sensed his deference to someone authorized to receive normally confidential information.

"I understand you're the bank officer who processed a loan application by Victor Talbert," I began. When he nodded, I asked him how much Talbert had wanted to borrow, and why.

McGregor unlocked a top desk drawer and pulled out some forms stapled together. He laid them on the desk and bowed his head to stare at them, the fingertips of his left hand touching his temple near his eye. He spoke without looking up, as if the forms intrigued him.

"Victor Talbert requested a loan of sixty thousand

dollars for capital to form a hardware distribution firm."

"Collateral?" I asked.

"The loan was to be granted in phases, secured by inventory."

"What made you decide against granting the loan?"

McGregor raised graying eyebrows in surprise. "But we didn't decide against. Talbert had an impeccable record, and his previous employer vouched for his integrity and ability. And my own personal assessment of Talbert was favorable. He was an impressive young man."

"Speaking as a nonbanker," I said, "it sounds risky."

"The phasing of the loan minimized the risk. In actuality we'd have been loaning the second half after the first had been paid. It was to be amortized over a ten-year period."

"Did he actually receive any money?"

"No, that's the strange thing about it. Talbert was contacted and told the directors had approved the loan. I talked to him myself. But on the date he was to come here to finalize the loan, he didn't show up."

"What day was that?"

McGregor traced a steady finger over the form before him. "The fifteenth of last month."

"What address did Talbert give you?"

The finger shot diagonally to the lower left corner of the form. "Five seventy Oakner, apartment seven."

I drew a folded slip of paper from my breast pocket and scribbled the information down. McGregor rotated the forms on the desk for my perusal in an exaggerated gesture of cooperation. I thumbed through them but saw nothing else useful. Talbert had listed himself as twenty-eight and single at the Oakner address. He'd had several employers before High Grade, but his experience was almost entirely in the hardware wholesaling business.

When I was finished, McGregor solicitously showed me out.

From First Security Trust I drove to the Oakner address Talbert had listed on his application, a tall brownstone apartment building set back on a narrow lot. Ivy was taking over the building's southeast corner, as if trying to bring the tall structure to earth.

I discovered what I'd expected. The apartment manager told me that Talbert had lived there for three months with a woman and young child, and when I showed him a photo of Joan Clark he identified her as the woman. They had moved out just over a month ago, without notice, but they had left behind an envelope containing the remainder of their rent money.

When I got back to the TraveLodge, I phoned Dockard and also got what information I expected from him. There were four men with major criminal records who used the name Robert Manners, either as their genuine name or an AKA—two in prison, one out of the country and the other eighty years old in a home in Iowa.

I replaced the receiver and stretched out on the bed, my shoes off, thinking about the day's main development. Keen, likable, admirable and ambitious Victor Talbert had run out on a sixty-thousand-dollar loan that would have enabled him to start his own business.

I found that remarkable.

14

I'd left word at the desk for a wake-up call at eight in the morning. When the phone rang it wasn't eight o'clock; it was three A.M. But it definitely woke me.

"*Somebody's hurt me! . . .*"

At first I didn't recognize the hysterical female voice.

"They beat me! . . ."

It was Belle Dee. "Belle, where are you?"

"Home . . . just got here. . . . They told me not to call the police. Said they'd kill me if I did. They kept asking about Vic. . . . I couldn't tell them any more than I told you!"

"I'll call a doctor."

"No! Please! A doctor might tell the police." The voice was still high, agonized, but she was gaining control.

I was responsible. I'd led somebody to her. "How badly hurt are you?"

"Don't know."

"I'll be there."

"Please, Alto! . . ."

"It's Alo," I said and hung up.

I was sitting on the edge of the bed, trembling, telling myself it was because the room was too cool. But I was scared. I reached for my pants.

The drive to Belle Dee's apartment was a skip in time, one of those chores performed automatically and precisely with the best part of the subconscious mind while the conscious boiled.

They'd done a job on her. She took a long time to answer my knock and reassurances, and when she inched open the door, she flinched in fright at the crack of light from the hall.

In the dimness of Belle Dee's apartment I could see that her upper lip was grotesquely swollen, and there was a slender track of blood down her neck, behind her right ear. She clung to me for a moment when I entered; then she slumped to the floor and sat against the wall, pressing the back of her head against the plaster, her eyes closed.

I switched on the softest light I could find, but she didn't like it. I didn't either. When I looked closely at the blood on her neck and the delicate splatter marks on her face, my stomach threatened and the room suddenly became an elevator going down.

"You all right?" she asked.

"I think so. Got any bandages?"

"Bathroom."

I found my way into the tile bathroom and opened the mirrored medicine chest. There was a bandage box, empty. But I found a roll of adhesive tape, some cotton, and on the vanity shelf beneath the washbasin an aerosol can of spray antiseptic.

Belle Dee was watching me, frantic-eyed, when I returned. "That stuff burns!"

"We'll use soap and water as much as possible," I said, helping her to her feet, then into a chair. Fighting off my dizziness, I went back to the bathroom and got some damp washrags and soap. Then I came back and did the best I could for her.

By the time I was finished, Belle Dee was leaning back in the chair, peering out at me from beneath a strip of tape over her right eyebrow. The eye was beginning to blacken. I got her some brandy, but it stung the cuts in her mouth, so she settled for ice water. I drank the brandy.

"How many were there?" I asked.

"Two. They were waiting for me when I came home. I shut the door, turned around and there they were."

"Do you know who they were?"

Belle Dee shook her head no. Her left hand was unconsciously clutching her stomach. She said they had kicked her. I was ashamed for being more frightened than angry.

"What did they say? What kind of questions did they ask you about Talbert?"

"They asked me how well I'd known him, if I had any idea who'd killed him, why Vic had left town. I told them I didn't know the answers. That got them mad, made them mean. They warned me not to answer any questions about Vic, from anyone, or they'd be back."

I poured another glass of brandy. "Could you identify them?"

"No, they wore something over their faces, like gauze."

"Nylon stockings?"

"Maybe. All I can tell you is, one of them had terrible breath." For an instant some inner pain etched twenty more years on her face. "Jesus! . . ."

"Sure you don't want a doctor?"

"I'd rather be hurt than dead."

There was my kind of logic. "Can you think of anybody who knew both you and Vic?" I asked.

"Nobody who'd do this. Just some of the people at the club, the other waitresses. They know him from when he'd come in to see me."

"Do you think Congram might be involved?"

"I only heard the name a few times, never met him. What's that?"

"Antacid tablet, for my stomach. Is there anybody who knew both Talbert and Congram?"

Her pain-filled eyes brightened. "Yeah, Vic once mentioned that Smit was involved with this Congram. That's been a while ago."

My heart picked up a beat. "Smit?"

"He's just a guy who comes into the club now and then—not so often anymore. Maybe once a week. A run-down looking guy who pops some kind of pills with his beer."

"How about a first name?"

Belle Dee licked her swollen lip and shook her head. "Smit's all I ever heard him called. One of the other waitresses used to go out with him, though. She might know his full name."

"And his address?"

"She might know. Unless he moved."

I finished the brandy, washing down the taste of the antacid tablet and gritting my teeth at the combination. "Can you find out for me tomorrow?"

She looked at me with her hurt doll's eyes and nodded. "I'll try."

I ran my fingertips over my stubbled chin and sighed. I was tired, and there was a knot of dread in my stomach. Joan Clark and Talbert had been mixed up with Congram, who knew Smit, who might lead me to trouble. Apparently Joan and Talbert had lived in the Oakner apartment before leaving unexpectedly for Florida. That must have been the apartment Melissa had described. I smiled as I remembered something else Melissa had said.

"Ever hear of Robert Manners?" I asked Belle Dee.

"No, why?"

"It probably isn't important. What about Gratuity Insurance?"

"Not that I can remember."

I walked into the kitchen and returned with one of the wooden chairs that had been at the table. "Wedge this under your doorknob when I leave," I told Belle Dee. "Then sometime tomorrow buy a chain lock."

She raised her head as if at a sudden sound. "You don't think they'll be back, do you?"

"No, I don t. They did their job. But you should have a chain lock anyway."

And Belle Dee's assailants had done their job

smoothly, probably slipping the apartment door lock with a credit card, then working swiftly and ruthlessly. There was no sign of a struggle.

I glanced at my watch and stood wearily before Belle Dee, waiting for her to invite me to spend the night. She didn't. So I cautioned her again to seal herself in, and left.

Back at my motel I wedged a chair under my own doorknob and had little success at sleeping. I had that uncomfortable feeling of being drawn into something I couldn't handle, and even thinking about the fifty thousand dollars didn't help.

I picked up the receiver on the first ring when Belle Dee called, a little after ten the same morning.

She told me where Smit lived and described him as a skinny, pinch-faced man in his thirties. She also warned me that Smit was involved in some kind of drug operation and had been arrested several times but never convicted.

That last part took away the possibility of breakfast. People involved in drug operations see life as being cheap.

15

The stench was the first thing that hit me. Stale sweat and the fetidness of something rotting.

Behind the half-open door a young girl stood staring blank-faced at me, unaware of the stench. She had narrow, bare and bony shoulders above a red halter that covered child's breasts. Her patched jeans appeared to be stained with grease. Behind her I could see a few pale faces in the dimness, some litter banked against one wall as if it had been swept there. The building was one of the few still occupied in a block of aged brick buildings that mercifully were due to be torn down.

"I'm looking for Smit," I told her. "There's money in it for him."

She laughed, spoke almost without moving her narrow lips. "What's he gotta do?"

"I'll talk to Smit about that."

"He ain't here anyway." The door closed.

I turned to walk down the graffiti-scrawled hall to the exit. A round peace symbol in fresh red paint had been brushed awkwardly over the door by somebody who hadn't heard we'd pulled out.

"You, Mister!"

My head jerked around to look behind me. A skinny, pinch-faced man in dark pants and a too-small sweater stood just outside the door the girl had closed. I waited and he walked toward me with that skinny man's ginger lightness in his step. He had protuberant dark eyes, curious despite fear.

"I'm Smit," he said.

"Nudger." I held out my hand and he shook it.

"So what do you want to talk to me about?"

As he spoke he was walking ahead of me, his head half turned, like a dog leading its master. He stopped when we were in the vestibule, where there was sunlight, cracked plaster and complete privacy.

"Congram," I said. "I'm not police and I'll pay."

I watched him think about it. The flesh of his slender face was mottled as he moved in a nervous little dance in the dust-swirled sunlight. From certain angles he was thirty-five, from others, fifty.

"Why do you want the information?" he asked and gnawed his lower lip as if he had something against it.

"Private matter."

Smit grinned and shook his head. I was aware of his gaunt hands, unafraid of him because of his slightness—as long as he didn't reach for a weapon.

"We're talking about a hundred dollars," I said.

The grin stretched, giving his face a cadaverous look. "Haven't you heard of the code of the underworld?"

"Two hundred dollars," I said, knowing Carlon would consider that cheap.

Smit's yellow grin contracted to a thin line, and he fondled a dimple on the point of his chin with a dirty forefinger.

"I can always say you talked anyway," I told him.

His face contorted as if he'd been stabbed. "Hey, Nudger, you wouldn't do that!" He began his nervous shuffle again.

"No," I said, "I wouldn't."

His nervous body was still. He'd come to a decision. "All right. It don't matter by now."

I placed a pair of hundred dollar bills in his skeletal, stained hands.

"How do I know this'll spend?" he asked, holding up the bills to the sunlight.

"How do I know you're going to tell me the truth?"

"Because I'm not going to tell you anything you can hang on Jerry. I don't know of anything."

Smit had already supplied me with a first name. I stood and waited for what else he had to say.

He nervously twisted the two bills into a cigarette-size roll and slipped them into his pocket. "I met Jerry at the Poptop Club, right after I got off on a possession charge. I guess that's how he found out about me and wanted to use me for an in on his business deal."

"Business deal?"

"This was over a year ago, understand. It can't do no

harm to tell now, or I wouldn t be telling it. Jerry wanted to buy into the middle of a connection; I don't exactly understand how. I think he was going to supply the capital to buy from the big dealer for a percentage of everything right down the line."

"How about some names?"

His eyes seem to contract in their sockets. "That I don't tell you, for any price. What I will say is that the operation no longer exists. It hasn't for almost a year. The law made some key busts and somebody knew when to quit. At least that's what I was told."

"Did you set it up for Congram to talk to the people involved?"

"Sure," Smit said with a hint of pride, "that I could do. But they turned Jerry down."

"For what reason?"

"They had no way to trust him. And it didn't help him being so clean-cut straight-city, hair above his ears and all that."

I waited for Smit to continue, there in the syrupy sunlight of the vestibule. A few cars passed outside, beyond the door's cracked glass, and in the distance a truck's air horn sounded three long notes. Smit crossed his arms over his sunken chest, squeezing in on himself nervously. He saw I wasn't satisfied.

"I was told you could be trusted," I said. He wondered who might have told me, and I wasn't about to tell him.

"Jerry tried to talk them into a deal," Smit said, "but they refused, and he finally gave up and forgot the idea. I ain't seen him since—almost a year. . . ."

"You brought Congram to the operation's attention," I said. "Didn't they ever ask you about him?"

"Sure. I told them what I told you. It was good enough."

I breathed out, loudly. "I'd have wanted to know more if I'd been them."

He uncrossed his arms and flexed his fingers, but he

didn't go into his dance. "Okay," he said, "they wanted to know where he lived, so once they had me follow him when he left the Poptop."

"Where did he lead you?"

"Hey, I don't remember the address! It's been a year!"

I drew another hundred of Carlon's money from my wallet.

"I'll have to take you there," Smit said, snapping the bill from my hand. "Money *is* the root of all evil, you know?"

"I'm not in any position to argue with you."

I drove the rental while Smit gave me directions, pointing the way with a lean and dirty-nailed finger. He sat leaning forward, pulled by his eagerness to be done with the unpleasantness of our agreement.

We didn't have to travel far, only out of the depressing, blighted area of the city and through the marginal neighborhoods that marked the boundary. I pulled to the curb where Smit told me to, and he pointed to a tall apartment building that had had a recent face-lift, up to the third floor only. EXECUTIVE TOWERS, a block-lettered sign proclaimed, a bit too grandly for the condition of the building.

"Which apartment?" I asked.

"I don't know," Smit said with almost desperate sincerity. "Only the building. . . . They had me follow him to the building, is all."

"What does Congram look like?" I asked.

"Hard to describe. Average height, build, nice-looking, nothing unusual about him except he's a great dresser. But there's something to him that tells you he's sharp."

"What color eyes?"

"Blue. His hair's dark and curly, cut short."

When there was a break in the traffic, I made a U-turn and drove Smit back to his own neighborhood and whatever his three hundred would buy. As he got out of the car, I assured him that our conversation would be kept confidential, but he knew there was no such thing and had the money in his pocket to prove it. He would worry for weeks, maybe months, in the shabby room where he lived with the thin, sad girl and whoever else slept there. Maybe he'd worry about our conversation for the rest of his life, as part of his collective worry. Some world.

I drove back to the Executive Towers.

The lobby of the face-lifted apartment building had also been remodeled recently. The walls seemed to be freshly painted, and the few cigarette butts and scuff marks were like a sacrilege on the gleaming red-and-white tile floor. I walked to the bank of brass mailboxes and scanned the name plates. No Congram. I pressed the button lettered MANAGER.

After a short wait I head a door open around a corner, and I walked toward the sound.

The manager's name was Toggins. He was a barrel-chested man wearing a leisure jacket and shirt open at the collar to reveal reddish hair that seemed to grope to reach his neck. He could have used that much hair on his head, bald but for some reddish strands combed sideways, like pencil lines, over his crown.

"I'm looking for Jerry Congram," I said. "I couldn't find his name on the mailboxes."

"No Congram lives here."

"Do you recall when he did?"

"Don't have to think hard to remember him," Toggins said. "Curly-haired young guy, nifty dresser. World by the tail."

"That's him."

"Moved out about four months ago without a forwarding address. And he still owes me three months on his lease." The barrel chest puffed out in resentment.

"Did he live here alone?"

"Ha! Signed the lease alone, but he always had company." Toggins smoothed the front of his shirt with an outspread hand, as if sensitive about his paunch. "Not the sort of company to cause trouble, though. Upstanding-looking young people, like from good homes. Course, Jerry Congram seemed that way, too, and he vamoosed without paying his rent."

"How many of these people would visit him at a time?"

"Sometimes seemed like a dozen, men and women. Never had any complaints, though. They were quiet types, like I said." He narrowed pink-rimmed eyes at me. "You ain't no friend of his, are you?"

"I'd like to find him, just like you."

"He owe you money?"

"You might say that." I reached into my wallet and got out a photo of Joan Clark. "This one of the young women who visited Congram?"

Toggins gave the snapshot his same narrow-eyed glare. "Yeah, sure is! She was in to see him all the time, like the rest of them. Hey, they didn't have anything goin' up there, did they?"

"Like what?"

"I don't know. You ain't a cop, are you?"

"No, a private detective."

Toggins backed up a step. "You puttin' me on? I never met one of you guys."

"There aren't many of us."

"If you find this Congram, will you let me know? Because of the rent."

"Sure. Did he keep pretty regular hours while he lived here?"

Toggins scratched the freckles on his forehead. "Well, that's pretty hard to say for sure, but he seemed to. Like I said, a typical clean-cut young guy, like you'd want your daughter to take up with. If I had what he does, I'd be doin' somethin' with it."

"How long had Congram lived here?"

"Nine months of a one-year lease." Toggins clamped a long cigar in his teeth and fired it up with a silver lighter. I wished he hadn't. The thick gray smoke that clouded the air around us gave off a pungent, sickening odor.

"Cherry-scented," he told me. "I smoke these and my wife don't bitch."

"Do you have any idea what Congram did for a living?" I asked him.

He did a George Burns with his cigar. "I couldn't say. He left here every day with his sharp suit and little briefcase. We got a lot of 'em here, captains of industry, if you know what I mean. I shouldn't be surprised when they skip out on their rent."

I told Toggins I appreciated his cooperation and got away from his cigar's fallout.

It had begun to rain, an insincere sort of drizzle from a half-blue sky. I stood for a while beneath the awning outside the Executive Towers, waiting for the rain to stop. The sidewalks were clear of people, and the tires of passing cars hissed on wet pavement. After Toggins' cigar, the rain-freshened air seemed especially sweet.

The deeper I delved into Talbert's murder and Joan Clark's disappearance, the more Congram emerged as a catalyst. I had no idea yet as to how he was involved, but I was almost certain of his involvement. Be it awe, envy or fear, the man had made an impression on everyone I'd talked to who'd known him.

The rain stopped as if it had been turned off, and I jogged across the bright, puddled street to my car.

I turned the ignition key and pulled out behind an old Ford full of teenagers. Most of the paint had been sanded from the Ford, giving it the appearance of a camouflaged military vehicle. I turned on my wipers to clear the windshield of raindrops and stopped behind the old Ford at a red light. Even a car-length behind I could hear the deep bass rhythm of the Ford's radio at

109

high volume. A miniature figure with outstretched arms and legs dangled by a thread or rubber band from the rearview mirror, like an obscene crucifix.

The traffic light flashed to green, and the Ford's tires whirred on wet cement. I didn't know why the driver was in such a hurry; there was a stop sign a block away.

The Ford braked to a nose-diving halt at the stop sign and had just stopped rocking when I pulled up behind it. Cross traffic had the intersection blocked for a few minutes, and I sat staring at the silhouetted, gently bobbing, spread-armed figure suspended from the Ford's rearview mirror. The dangling figure loosened something on the edge of my memory, and suddenly that something illuminated into image in my mind—the image of a newspaper photograph, a man in a dark business suit, plummeting to his death, limbs outstretched and body arced as if in a last desperate and maniacal attempt to soar. A man the photo's caption had identified as Robert Manners.

Dale Carlon had been examining the newspaper in the Star Lane house, but he'd been concerned mainly with the idea of a top business executive's pressures driving him to suicide, relating the story to his own problems. So he hadn't remembered the man's name, as I hadn't until my memory had been flicked by the sight of the dangling rearview mirror ornament. And Robert Manners was the name penciled on the back of a business card lettered GRATUITY INSURANCE. "Ingerence," as Melissa Clark had mispronounced it.

I tried to remember some details of the story. Manners had been a Los Angeles business executive, member of a long list of boards and committees. Had he been depressed over something specific? Had he left any family? I couldn't remember.

I stopped at a service station and got directions to the Chicago Public Library, at Michigan and Washington.

The Chicago papers had carried the Robert Manners story on the same date as the Layton paper. The library had it on microfilm. Manners had been district manager of a big firm called Witlow Cable, the exact business of which wasn't stated. He had leaped to his death from the roof of Witlow Cable's twelve story office building. Business associates said he had been unusually tense lately, though the business was going well. And Manners' widow reported that he had seemed depressed lately, but not to the point of suicide. No note had been found, but Manners' personal effects had been removed from his pockets and arranged neatly on a corner of his desk. Police had no reason to suspect foul play but were investigating.

I leaned back from the microfilm viewer. I knew how the police investigated that sort of case. How much time and manpower did they have to waste on a violent death that was almost certainly a suicide? Not all of the troubled who choose their own time to leave this world are considerate enough to leave behind notes of explanation.

Back at my motel, I looked in the Chicago telephone directory for a Gratuity Insurance. There was none listed. I phoned a few national insurance organizations for information about Gratuity, but as far as they could determine there was no such company.

The direction I had to take was clear. West to Los Angeles, the City of Angels. I didn't like that allusion to an afterlife.

I got in touch with Dale Carlon and brought him up to date on developments. He said that at the Star Lane house he'd been interested in the Layton paper's photo and news account of Manners' death because of the business-pressure angle, the presumed motive for suicide. Everyone involved in high level decision-making had felt that pressure, Carlon told me, including himself. The prospect of suicide was considered, if only fleetingly, by many who shouldered such responsi-

111

bility. It was difficult for me to imagine someone as wealthy and self-serving as Carlon contemplating suicide, but bearing in mind the fifty thousand dollars, I didn't tell him that.

He did agree with me that it was now hard to believe the newspaper's being folded to that page at the Star Lane house was coincidental. Either the paper was deliberately left arranged that way or, more likely, someone had been reading the account of Manners' death with interest and had put down the paper still folded to the story.

Carlon also agreed that the answers to some of our questions were in Los Angeles and that I should travel there immediately. He would spare no expense to find his daughter. He would spare no one.

16

The weather wasn't good in Los Angeles. The city was in the midst of a heat wave combined with a thick layer of smog.

By one o'clock, when I arrived at Witlow Cable in downtown L.A. for the appointment Carlon had set up for me, the sun had burned away most of the smog, but the heat remained. Witlow Cable's headquarters were frigidly air-conditioned, though, and I was only inside the building for about five minutes before I found myself almost longing to be back out on the street.

A pertly sweet secretary informed me that I could see Mr. Brian Cheevers, and she ushered me into an office that was nothing if not sumptuous. A royal-blue carpet I found myself wading in stretched to mirrored walls and thick, paler blue ceiling-to-floor drapes. A white sofa with blue throw pillows sat against the wall on my right, and there were matching white chairs before an enormous desk of bleached wood trimmed in blue.

Behind the desk Mr. Brian Cheevers, a squat, swarthy man with a lumpy face and hungry eyes, stood to shake my hand. His appearance was civilized somewhat by the elegant suit disguising the powerful bulk of his shoulders.

He motioned me into one of the exquisite, soft white chairs in front of his desk, and I sat with the feeling that I was deflowering a virgin.

"You want to talk about Bob Manners," he said, as if planting the thought in my mind.

"I won't take much of your time, Mr. Cheevers. I want to know primarily about the time leading up to Manners' death."

"I notice you didn't say suicide."

"I try to keep an open mind. Do you have any opinion on whether or not it was suicide?"

"No, I don't worry about it. It's passed. Manners is dead. I leave that sort of speculation to the proper authorities."

The no-nonsense mind in action, I thought. Too busy to be curious about the death of an associate. On the other hand, Cheevers might have an hour each day scheduled for curiosity. I cautioned myself against judging too harshly.

"Did you know Manners well?" I asked.

"He was my immediate superior for five years," Cheevers said with vaguely military overtones.

"According to the newspapers, fellow employees said that business pressures had upset Manners for several weeks before his death. Can you tell me what sort of pressures?"

113

Cheevers picked up a gold pen and held it gently, as if it were a royal scepter. "There are always great pressures being brought to bear in this job, Mr. Nudger, as there were in the period immediately preceding Bob Manners' death. I will say he seemed unusually tense at the time, but if that tenseness was the result of business pressure, it had to have been accumulative."

"What about pressures from his home life?"

Cheevers' lumpy face twisted into a slight grin. "Not with that wife of his. Elizabeth is the perfectly trained executive's wife. I don't think I'm maligning the man by saying that Manners would never have attained his position without her."

"Didn't Manners ever talk to you . . . on a personal basis?"

"Not often. He never gave me any idea what was causing his apprehension, and I didn't consider it my business."

"Was there anyone here he might have confided in?"

"I doubt it. Bob Manners was all business. He didn't believe in confiding his personal problems to his subordinates, and everyone here was a subordinate."

"Do you know of anyone else, outside the business, he might have talked to about his problems?"

Cheevers shook his head. "Manners' career was his life. On this level, that's the way it has to be." He pretended to sneak a glance at his watch.

I hung on. "Has Witlow Cable ever done business with Gratuity Insurance?"

"No." Cheevers' answer was immediate and confident.

"What about when Manners was in charge?"

"I'd have known about it." Cheevers' manner was as cool and unruffled as the office decor. Behind him the sun beat futilely on the tall window. "I'm a bit pressed for time, Mr. Nudger. Is there anything else?"

"Yes, I'd like to talk to Manners' secretary."

He seemed to consider the reasonableness of that for a moment. "All right," he said. "Her name's Alice Kramer. She's in accounting now." He picked up the white receiver from the phone on his desk and punched one of a row of buttons. "Bernie, Cheevers. A man named Nudger is coming down to talk to Alice about Bob Manners. Tell her to cooperate." Cheevers hung up the phone, apparently without waiting for a reply.

I stood and shook hands with him again and slow-bounded over the deep carpet toward the door.

"By the way," I said as I was going out, "what exactly does Witlow Cable produce"

"Industrial cable, petroleum storage tanks and carpet," he said. I shouldn't have been surprised.

The secretary who had ushered me into Cheevers' office gave me directions to accounting, on the second floor. I took an elevator down and followed a long hall to a wooden door with ACCOUNTING lettered on it in neat black print. The door was locked. I turned left with the hall, glanced into a large empty employee's cafeteria, then came to another door, open. I stepped inside to see a small gray-haired woman savagely putting an electric typewriter through its paces.

"Accounting?" I asked.

She nodded without breaking rhythm.

"Alice Kramer?"

"She's waiting for you in there," the mad typist said, jerking her head toward a door on her left as the type-writer's margin bell chimed.

I walked through the door and was in a small green-walled room with two chairs and a low table with a lamp on it. It was the sort of room used only for heart-to-hearts, and I could sense that it was haunted by many a departed accountant. In one of the chairs sat a neatly dressed, attractive woman in her mid-forties. Her dark brown hair was short and disciplined; her smile was pleasant but harried. After introductions, we got to the subject of her ex-boss.

"I've been told Manners was the all-business type," I said to her, slipping into the other chair, "so as his secretary you were probably closer to him than anyone else in the company."

She nodded briskly, conceding the truth in that.

"Did you notice any tenseness, any apprehension in him before his death?"

"Everyone did," she said in a carefully modulated but warm voice. "Not that he behaved in such a way that it would sound extravagant, or even unusual, if described; but it was the contrast. Before that time Mr. Manners was one of the most even-tempered men you could meet, always considerate and genuinely concerned with other people. Then suddenly he became . . . grim, constantly drawn into himself."

"And he never told you why?"

"No. You were right in assuming Mr. Manners put more trust in me than in anyone else here, but our relationship was still one of employer to employee. He kept his personal problems to himself."

"How long before his death did you first notice the change in him?"

She crossed her long legs primly, folded her arms. "I'm sure I was the one who first noticed a change, about two months . . . before. Then other people began to notice that he always seemed preoccupied, which wasn't at all like Mr. Manners. Approximately a week before . . . it happened he became increasingly agitated, depressed." Her eyes took on the sheen of suppressed tears. "I asked him what was bothering him, if I could help, but he said not to worry about him, that things would work out."

I didn't like wringing her, but I had to. I was getting a lump in my own throat. "Were you here at work when he died?"

Alice relinquished just enough self-control to brush at her eyes with a long-nailed forefinger. "I was at my desk. Mr. Manners came out of his office and walked past me without speaking, but he seemed quite normal. He must have gone directly to take the service elevator to the roof. Ten minutes later I was told that he'd fallen."

"Fallen?"

"Suicide wasn't considered at the time. The police put that theory together later."

"But you don't believe it?"

Her entire body seemed to stir in a weary shrug. "I don't know. Something *was* disturbing him. . . ."

"What do you think of Mrs. Manners?"

"I like her. At first I didn't; I thought she was too . . . pushy. Then I came to realize that she was totally dedicated to her husband's career. I saw her make many sacrifices over the past several years."

"Were you friends with her?"

"Not exactly. I think she knew her husband might not want that."

The low hum of an air conditioner or ventilator fan, which I don't think either of us was aware of, suddenly stopped, leaving a somehow louder silence in the tiny room. Alice Kramer spoke again, quickly, as if to keep the silence from engulfing us.

"Are you investigating his death?"

"Only indirectly."

"Then why? . . ."

"I'm investigating a disappearance, Miss Kramer. Have you ever heard the name Victor Talbert?"

"I don't think so."

"Jerry Congram?"

"No."

"Gratuity Insurance?"

She hesitated. "No . . . not that I can recall."

I watched her reach into her purse, which leaned

117

against the leg of her chair, and draw out a pack of cigarettes. She offered me one and I declined. Her lean fingers trembled as she held a dainty gold lighter's flame to the tobacco.

"Do you think Mrs. Manners would talk to me?" I asked. "You could phone, tell her who I am."

"I'm sure she'd see you," Alice said, drawing on her cigarette as if trying to collapse it. I could see she smoked for medicinal purposes.

I stood and held the door open for her, then sat back down and watched through the still-open door as she used the phone on the typist's desk to call Mrs. Manners. I couldn't hear what she was saying, didn't particularly want to. Now and then she'd glance over at me as she talked.

After a few minutes Alice hung up the phone and walked to the doorway. "She can see you at four o'clock today."

I stood and thanked her. The expression on her face told me no thanks were necessary. She was still loyal, doing a last service for her ex-boss.

The four o'clock appointment with Mrs. Manners left me some spare time, but not much. I decided to have a late lunch in the employee's automatic cafeteria I'd noticed down the hall, then drive directly to see Elizabeth Manners.

The cafeteria was still empty. The center of the room was filled with small round tables and metal-legged plastic chairs, and the walls were lined with vending machines that dispensed soup, sandwiches and desserts. Next to a coffee machine, in a corner, was a small microwave oven on a table under a sign that read KEEP OUR LUNCH ROOM CLEAN.

After only a moderate struggle, I managed to coax one of the sandwich machines to accept my money and part with a ham and cheese sandwich. But the soda machine worked with clicking, whirring perfection

118

and winked at me as I withdrew the cup. I sat at a table near a corner and peeled the cellophane from my sandwich. After a few bites I noticed the piped-in music, as bland as the food.

When I'd finished eating, I dutifully threw my debris into one of the trash containers placed about the cafeteria; then I got a cup of black coffee from the machine near the microwave oven and sat back down to try to relax.

The coffee wasn't bad for machine coffee, and I lingered over it. Two young office girls came in and regarded me as just another machine while they traded dimes for chewing gum, then left. Other than that I drank my coffee alone; then I leaned back in my chair and idly rotated the empty plastic cup on the tabletop.

"I did it just the opposite," a female voice said behind me. "I saw Mrs. Manners first."

A statement like that in a room I'd thought empty wasn't the sort of surprise I liked.

I turned in my chair.

17

She was a tall, auburn-haired woman in her early thirties, clear-complexioned, leanly well built and with carefully penciled, arched eyebrows that gave her a sharp eyed, inquisitive expression. "I'm Alison Day of *Business View*," she said, "and you're Alan Nudger."

"Alo," I corrected her, "but how did you come so close?"

She smiled an all-knowing, sharkish smile that had a curious sexual appeal to it. Her features were of a sharpness that would have been unattractive but for their chiseled perfection. "I'm a feature writer for my magazine, researching for a series of articles on the pressures and unexplained suicides and accidental deaths of top business executives across the country. You came here to Witlow Cable and now plan to go interview Mrs. Elizabeth Manners; I did things the opposite. I've talked to Robert Manners' widow, and now, here I am at Witlow. I was just getting ready to leave Mrs. Manners when her husband's secretary phoned. I asked about the call and Elizabeth Manners told me about your appointment. Though I thought you might be gone from here, I decided to check anyway. And here we are."

"Why?"

She appeared surprised. "What?"

"Why are we here? Why did you want to see me?"

"Oh, I wanted to find out about your involvement in this, of course." She spotted my empty cup, then the coffee machine. There was a boldness in her lean-legged stride as she crossed the cafeteria to the vending machine. She reached into her purse and pulled out some change. "Can I buy you another coffee?"

"Thanks, no. I don't want to make a pig of myself, and a chauvinistic one at that."

She gave me the knowing, eyes-sideways smile to show I hadn't rattled her. I took an antacid tablet.

"We can help each other, I think . . . Aldo, is it?"

"Alo."

"Call me Alison. You're a private detective. That's really fascinating."

"It's all in the eye of the fascinatee. What did Mrs. Manners tell you, Alison?"

"She said that her husband had seemed worried about something for months before his death, but that he never told her exactly about what. When she pressed him on the subject, he would simply categorize his worries as business pressures. I find this recent trend curious because the suicide rate among top executives is well below the national average. Statistically, six-point-six percent—"

"Alison," I interrupted her, holding up my palm in the universal stop signal, "I am not a believer in statistics."

"Really?" She sipped the coffee she'd bought and strode back to my table. "I should think you would be, being in a sense a policeman. Given sufficient and accurate data, statistics are an invaluable tool, in the business world especially. More sales are generated—"

I held up my hand again. "I'm not interested in sales being generated," I told her. "I've got too much on my mind as it is. Is that all that Manners' widow told you?"

She stared down at me with amused eyes that were a cattish pale green. "Essentially, yes." She smiled. "What did Brian Cheevers tell you?"

"So we can cross check their stories?"

She nodded, still smiling. She had a good idea. I gave her most of what Cheevers had told me.

"There is one thing," I said as she sat across from me, mentally digesting what I'd told her. "I can't promise to tell you everything; I have certain obligations you don't."

"Sure, I understand that. I never thought you trusted me completely, either. Who are you working for?"

I had a vision, then, of her descending on Dale Carlon, using my name, spouting her *Business View* facts and figures at him in her crisp, confident tone. Then the questions. I guessed Alison Day might be the last representative of the press Carlon would want to know about his missing daughter.

"I have to keep that confidential for the time being," I said to her.

She appeared disappointed but not surprised. I was

becoming more wary of her by the minute. I said, "You mentioned something about the deaths of several top executives across the country. . . ."

"Yes," Alison said, "counting Manners, six, nationwide, in a very short period of time."

"I wasn't aware of the trend."

"One would have to be in a position to see the entire cloth to discern the pattern."

"And your magazine thinks there is a pattern?"

She lowered her coffee cup from her lips. "That's partly what I've been assigned to discover."

I wadded my own cup and tossed it neatly into a trash container. I didn't like the idea of becoming mixed up with a reporter, but at this point there was little to lose. She had no idea who or what I was actually investigating, and I could keep it on those terms.

"Have you ever heard of the Gratuity Insurance Company?" I asked her.

"No, why?"

"I wondered if anyone you've questioned in connection with the other deaths mentioned them."

"No, but on the other hand, I didn't ask. I can check back, though."

I smiled at her. "That's what I was really asking."

Alison pulled a notebook from her purse. "Gratuity Insurance," she said, jotting it down as she pronounced it.

"How about the name Jerry Congram?" I asked while she had her notebook out. The pencil darted again while Alison spelled the name aloud to me.

She looked at me expectantly for a moment saw nothing else was forthcoming and snapped the notebook shut. "I'm at the Clairbank Hotel," she said, "room four oh seven. That's an invitation only to exchange information after you've talked to Elizabeth Manners and I've talked to Brian Cheevers."

"I thought you might want to show me your stock market graphs," I said innocently.

She looked at me with something like genuine disgust. "Can you be there about seven?"

"I'll try. We can discuss things over dinner, but only because I'll be hungry."

We left the lunchroom to keep our respective appointments, walking together to the elevator.

As I passed from the cool lobby into fierce heat outside I was trying to decide whether the advent of Alison Day would prove a hindrance or a help. Then I realized there was no way to make that decision until I determined that there actually was a connection between the deaths of Robert Manners and Victor Talbert.

If no connection existed, Alison Day wouldn't matter, and I'd have to try to pick up the thread of the investigation in Chicago.

18

Elizabeth Manners lived in a sun-faded but stately neo-Spanish home not far off the Ventura Freeway. Azaleas were thriving along the wide front of the pastel yellow house, and as I rang the doorbell I could see a curved garden path flanked by rhododendrons, some of them still displaying rosy-purple blooms.

Mrs. Manners answered the door almost immediately. When I identified myself, she smiled at me and held the door open wider. She was a very thin, graceful woman, somewhere in her sixties, with the sort of beauty that retains its gentle magnetism far into old age. Her face was lined but taut, and her thin frame was draped in a simple but expensive purple dress. If one word were needed to describe her, it would be "gracious."

She endured my clumsy expressions of sympathy, then led me to a room of pinks and blues that had been blessed by a decorator's touch. After I'd declined her offer of something to drink, we sat to talk.

"Have you any idea what was bothering your husband?" I asked her.

Her folded hands, strangely older than the rest of her, lay, withered yet elegant, in her lap. "No, Mr. Nudger, Robert didn't share that problem with me, which was uncharacteristic."

"Why do you think he chose not to confide in you?"

"I don't know. One of the reasons I agreed to talk to you and the young lady is my curiosity about that matter. Robert and I were close; we worked together for his career."

"But you agree with the consensus that he was depressed."

"I would describe it more as anxious, apprehensive." She frowned as she sifted for explanations. "Perhaps he was afraid for me to know why."

"Do you think it was something connected with his work?"

"I doubt it. As I said, we worked together for his career." The withered hands in her lap shifted, briefly separated, as if seeking some purpose, then folded back into each other.

"Do you think, in the week or so before your husband's death, that his apprehension grew, reached a peak?"

"To the point of driving him to suicide?"

She was trying to make my tact unnecessary. "Well, yes."

"I think that's apparent, Mr. Nudger."

"Then you believe it was suicide?"

"I know it." Something in her pale eyes turned inward for a second, surveying her thoughts. "I'm going to tell you something I chose not to tell the young lady and I'd like you to keep it confidential unless you absolutely must reveal it. Only under those terms will I tell you, and then I'll tell you only because you are the only representative of the law still investigating my husband's death, and I'd like to know why he elected to die. Miss Day is a magazine writer, and I do not want my husband to become a case in point in some article, an example."

"I can understand that," I told her, "and I can promise you."

She looked at me for a long moment, her hands still. Then she stood and walked to a dainty walnut secretary desk near the white-curtained window. She drew an envelope from one of the flat drawers and handed it to me.

"My husband's suicide note," she said in a voice detached from emotion. "It was delivered in the mail the day after he died."

I accepted the white envelope, examined the postmark. "Do the police know about this?"

"No one has known about it but me, and now you."

Elizabeth Manners sat back down as I drew the neatly typed, folded paper from the envelope and read.

Dearest Elizabeth:

I die by my own hand because I know this to be my wisest alternative—indeed my duty. I have never balked at responsibility, nor would you want me to even now if you could know the circumstances.

I am grateful for all that you have been to me, saddened to cause you this necessary pain.

Your loving husband forever,
Robert

125

The letter was signed beneath a typed signature, a distinctive black-inked scrawl.

"Is this your husband's signature?" I asked.

Elizabeth Manners nodded. "I have no doubt of that, Mr. Nudger."

I replaced the letter in its envelope and handed it back to her. "Why haven't you given this to the police?"

She leaned forward in her chair with a strangely graceful, compelling intensity. "I knew if the police learned my husband had definitely killed himself they would stop investigating his death. And I wanted to know *why* he committed suicide." She leaned back, smiled a sadly resigned smile. "I see now that it made no difference; the police are no longer concerned with the case anyway. They've accepted the theory of Robert's suicide, like everyone else."

"And it would be pointless to tell them about the letter now," I said.

"Exactly. You are a private detective, Mr. Nudger. Would you consider undertaking to find the reason for my husband's death? Obviously you already have some interest in doing this or you wouldn't have talked to Brian Cheevers and Alice. So I would like to hire you."

I shook my head. "That won't be necessary, Mrs. Manners. What you want coincides with what I'm presently investigating, and if I find out anything I'll be glad to let you know."

"I insist on paying."

"We'll talk about that if the time comes," I told her. "In the meantime, maybe you can help. Did your husband ever mention the Gratuity Insurance Company?"

"No, I never heard of them."

"The names Jerry Congram or Victor Talbert?"

"Neither of them are familiar."   \

An evenly spaced, relentless thudding and scraping

sound came from outside the window, a sound that seemed to violate the quietly tasteful and orderly room.

"My gardener," Mrs. Manners explained.

I recognized then the sound of a hoe being worked in soft earth. "Do you know who, at Witlow Cable, profited the most from your husband's death?"

"Brian Cheevers, although I doubt that at the time he knew he would profit."

Unless he'd known something Mrs. Manners hadn't. Cheevers was definitely the close-to-the-vest type. I didn't want to think that Manners' death might be unrelated to whatever his connection was with Gratuity Insurance, but it was a possibility. The problem was that there were a number of unrelated possibilities.

"Who was your husband's doctor, Mrs. Manners?"

"Steiner, on Hobart Avenue. I asked him about my husband. He said Robert had been in perfect health except for high blood pressure that could easily have been remedied."

I sat back, crossed my outstretched legs at the ankles and thought about Robert Manners—a man in good health, near the top of his profession, and with a dedicated wife whom he obviously loved. When a man like that committed suicide, it was usually brought on by something outside his normal sphere of existence, something often impossible to discover. I didn't envy Elizabeth Manners her quest, and I couldn't look with optimism on my own task.

Outside the gardener continued his toil, each *chunk* of the hoe like something breaking off and lost forever. Elizabeth Manners seemed impervious to the sound.

I assured her I could find my own way out and left her there.

From the Manners home I went to see Dr. Steiner, on Hobart Avenue.

His office was in one of those quasi-hospital medical

centers equipped to do everything but bury the patient. It was a white-brick building with few windows and an arrowed sign explaining that the emergency entrance was around the back.

Happy to use the front entrance, I walked across a large reception area lined with red-vinyl sofas and low tables spread with dog-eared magazines. Everything but the magazines seemed new, slickly and professionally done, and there was a toy-and-game-equipped alcove off the reception area for the children to play in as they waited.

Half a dozen people were seated about the room, ignoring each other—two elderly men and four women. One of the women had on a low-cut dress she could have worn anywhere, another a heavy, jeweled necklace that soaked up most of the light in the room.

Behind a long, curved counter several white-uniformed women were moving about with smooth efficiency, and as I approached, one of them, a severe-looking young darkhaired girl, asked if she could help me.

I told her I'd like to talk to Dr. Steiner.

"Do you have an appointment?"

"No," I said, "it has to do with one of his patients."

"The doctor's very busy right now."

"I can wait for a while."

"He has a full schedule today."

The nurse, or whatever her title was, was beginning to annoy me. No doubt part of her job was to protect Dr. Steiner from pesty private detectives and medical supply salesmen, but I did wish she'd let him know I was there.

"I only need a few minutes of the doctor's time," I told her, careful to hide my growing irritation. "My name is Nudger, Alo Nudger. Would you tell him I'm here?"

She neither moved nor dropped her professionally detached manner. "If you'd tell me the nature of your business. . . ."

"It's private."

"Concerning which patient?"

"Mr. Robert Manners."

She pardoned herself and turned her back on me to riffle through a long, slender drawer of indexed three-by-five cards. There was something about her squarish hips and broad waist. Even from behind she looked intractable.

"I can find no Robert Manners," she said, sliding the long file drawer shut as she turned again to face me.

"Who am I talking to?" I asked.

"Nurse Malloy."

"Nurse Malloy, will you do me a favor and tell Dr. Steiner I'm here, and that it concerns Robert Manners and that it's important."

She glared at me with cool disinterest, as if she'd tired of toying with me and had more important things to do. "I checked. I'm sure the doctor has no such patient, Mr. Nudger."

"Manners is dead," I told her, my voice taking on ice. "And I'm sure Dr. Steiner wouldn't like it if he knew you were preventing me from talking to him about that unpleasant fact."

She stared at me as I were inanimate yet thought-provoking. "I'll inform the doctor," she said with distaste. "You should realize I'm only performing my duties. If everyone who came in here wanting to see one of the doctors was allowed to go in without first establishing a good reason, there'd be little time to care for the patients."

I didn't like the implication that I and people like me were somehow a threat to the proper medical care of the ill, but I said nothing as Nurse Malloy turned and disappeared through a doorway behind the curved counter. The two other women behind the counter continued their work and ignored me.

Almost five minutes passed before the nurse returned.

"Dr. Steiner can give you a few minutes," she said. Then her face brightened as if the sun had struck it, and she looked past me. "Mrs. Nesmith!" she said in a pleased voice. "You're here to pick up your medicine." The very old woman who was Mrs. Nesmith shuffled forward and basked in Nurse Malloy's good cheer. I saw that it helped to be a paying customer.

Dr. Steiner invited me into a small, antiseptic room with a sterile white washbasin and a leather-upholstered table covered with something resembling butcher paper.

Steiner looked like an expensive doctor—stocky, middle-aged, with heavy-lidded, serious eyes and a brush mustache. It was easy to imagine him in a laboratory somewhere, a microscope-glance away from some major medical breakthrough.

"Nurse Malloy tells me you're interested in Robert Manners," he said. "I am busy, Mr. Nudger. . . ."

"What I'm interested in, Doctor, is the state of Manners' health preceding his suicide."

"I see." A cautious note had entered his voice. "Who do you represent?

"No one directly connected with Robert Manners. The information I'm seeking is only incidental to the case I'm on."

I could see he didn't believe me. "I'm sorry," he said with a smile. "Professional ethics forbid me to divulge a patient's medical history without permission."

"I'm not exactly asking you to do that, Doctor. Can you just tell me if Manners' medical state prior to his death might have caused him to commit suicide?"

Dr. Steiner gave my question a lot of thought, thick

eyebrows lowered in a superb bedside frown. Maybe he was worried about a malpractice suit.

"I've already talked to Mrs. Manners," was all he said.

"So have I."

"Then I assume you know the answer to your question." He gave me a good-bye smile. "As you saw in the reception area, we have several patients to be served."

And in the income bracket not to be kept waiting, I thought as he stepped smoothly aside to let me exit first.

I left Dr. Steiner's hoping my health would last forever.

Outside the medical center I made a few phone calls from a public booth, trying to get in touch with an old friend of mine, Lieutenant Sam Hiller, of the Los Angeles police.

Hiller was off duty, but I contacted him at his home, and he told me to drive in to see him and gave me directions.

It would be good to see Hiller, I thought, getting back into my car. We'd worked together for a while, until he decided to go with the Los Angeles Police Department because it had the reputation of being the best and most demanding of its officers. That was the sort of situation Hiller craved.

Then, six years ago, Hiller was shot while attempting to quiet a family disturbance, and five months of hospitalization and three operations changed him. He eased up somewhat, on himself and everyone around him. I'd gotten along with the old Hiller, but the new Hiller was much more pleasant company.

He lived in a condominium unit in one of those sprawling low projects that look like luxury military barracks. The slant-roofed two-story buildings were lined along a wide cement walkway punctuated by

131

potted trees and ornate lampposts. A young boy was repeatedly running at one of the metal posts, gripping it and letting his momentum swing him in circles.

My knock on Hiller's door was answered by a call to come in.

The room was neatly and symmetrically arranged, clean, without clutter—books lined precisely on their shelves, lamp shades and pictures as straight as if they'd been adjusted with levels. Hiller himself was sitting with his stockinged feet propped on a hassock, watching the Dodger game on television. I was struck, as I had been before, by how he maintained his uncompromising perfectionist's attitude toward things but not toward people.

He stood and shook my hand, got us each a beer and told me to have a seat on the couch.

"They don't bunt," he said, settling back into his chair. "Ballplayers nowadays can't bunt." He looked older than when I'd last seen him, had less hair and more loose flesh beneath his jutting jaw.

Together we watched an attempted sacrifice bunt result in a sickly pop fly to the third baseman. Hiller shook his head in disgust.

"What are you onto, Nudger?" he asked.

"I need to know something about a suicide here," I said without directly answering his question, knowing he wouldn't push. "A big businessman named Robert Manners."

Hiller sat still for a while, eyes fixed on the TV. "I recall it, but I don't know much about it."

I sipped my cold beer. "There probably isn't much to know, but Manners' doctor was no help. I thought I might be able to check the autopsy report and whatever else is available through you."

"Sure."

The third out was a near home run. Hiller groaned, excused himself and left the room. I heard him talking on the telephone in the hall. He was on the phone for a long time. When he came back to the living room, he was carrying two more cans of the very cold beer.

"What happened, Nudger?"

"Strikeout, walk, double play," I said, accepting the chilled wet can. "What happened where you were?"

"Probably a strikeout there, too. The autopsy report on Manners says he was in good health until he hit the sidewalk. And a subsequent investigation turned up nothing to suggest his death was anything but suicide."

I nodded, took a pull on my beer in disappointment.

"There is one thing, though," Hiller said. "I talked to the officer who handled the investigation. For what it's worth, he says a suicide finding didn't sit quite right with him, but it was only a feeling. The facts said suicide."

I understood what Hiller was saying, but I also knew how often hunches were wrong. "Is the case still being actively investigated?"

Hiller stared at me "You know better than that. Time, money and manpower come into it. They don't let us go looking for crime when there's no live victim and there are far to many live victims walking around out there today."

Hiller had a point I couldn't contradict.

"Stick around for a while," he invited. "Watch the ball game. It's a genuine pitchers' duel."

"For an inning or so," I said. "I've got an appointment later at a hotel with a beautiful girl."

Hiller laughed. "As long as no money changes hands." He propped his feet on the hassock again.

When I left him to drive to the Clairbank, the Dodgers had just scored three runs on a triple, and he was happy.

The Clairbank was one of L.A.'s older hotels, spacious and accommodating, the sort that still offers top service at moderate rates. I crossed the carpeted lobby, took a smooth but slow elevator to the fourth floor and knocked on the door of 407.

"You're late," Alison said as she opened the door.

"And hungry," I told her, glancing at my watch to see that it was five after seven. "Why don't we talk things over while we're having dinner downstairs?"

Alison must not have eaten, either, because she agreed, stepped into the hall and closed the door behind her. She was wearing a pale-green outfit with a loose-fitting skirt and chunky, thick-soled shoes, which, despite the work of a deranged fashion designer, failed to rob her ankles of their grace.

The Clairbank had a comfortable restaurant with good food and a varied menu. Over chicken oreganata specials, we discussed.

"What did Elizabeth Manners tell you?" Alison asked, sipping her wine.

"That her husband committed suicide," I said truthfully, but stopped short of mentioning the letter. "He'd been apprehensive for some time, then especially so just before his death."

"Do you think she really believes it was suicide?"

"I'm sure she does. And I'm sure she'll never get over it."

"You might be right. This sauce is terrific."

I watched her use her knife and fork enthusiastically on her chicken breast. She bothered me. She was one of the few women whom I felt I should dislike but who greatly appealed to me. I considered trying to work out a way to spend the night in the Clairbank, in room 407. Maybe it was something in the sauce.

"Okay," she said, "let's compare notes on Mr. Brian Cheevers."

Cheevers had told her, almost word for word, what he'd told me. Alison had also gotten a duplicate story from Manners' secretary, Alice Kramer. Not much on the West Coast had panned out.

134

"So we learned nothing," Alison said, with some dejection, to her half-consumed chicken breast. "There was nothing unusual or business-related about Manners' suicide."

For some reason I felt I had to console her. "Either that or everyone has his story memorized to perfection."

She looked up at me. "Do you suppose that's possible, some sort of conspiracy?"

I understood why she was a reporter. Some of the juiciest news is wished into being.

"You know anything's possible," I told her.

Alison waited until we'd got to the rice pudding before saying, "Oh, incidentally, I found something on your Gratuity Insurance. I phoned the secretary of Craig Blount, a high-level executive killed in a hit-and-run accident a few weeks ago in Seattle. She told me she remembered that some time ago a man from Gratuity had called at the office and seemed to upset her boss tremendously."

"Upset him how?"

"Made him edgy and bad-tempered," Alison said, "which wasn't like him."

Good as the food was, my fluttering stomach would accept no more. I set my fork down and sat back in my chair.

"What's the matter?" she asked.

"The thing about Gratuity Insurance," I told Alison, "is that there is no such company."

19

The next day I knocked again on Elizabeth Manners' door. When I got no answer I looked about and found her in the garden, with a pruning shears, working on an espaliered lemon tree. She turned, startled, as she heard my footsteps on the path.

"Mr. Nudger!" she said with what seemed to be genuine pleasure. "I hope you've returned because you've discovered something."

"Maybe a crack of light, Mrs. Manners." It was peaceful in the garden, pleasantly shaded. I hated to pull Elizabeth Manners into the subject of her husband's death.

"Gardening pacifies the soul," she said, working the red-handled shears expertly; but I could see her tenseness as she waited for what I had to say.

"Was your husband acquainted with any of these business executives?" I asked, feeling somewhat like the serpent in the garden. I read her the list of five names given to me by Alison.

Mrs. Manners continued to work the shears for a while before answering. Then she lowered them to her side and faced me. "Craig Blount. I don't think they were acquainted, but I remember the morning Robert and I were having breakfast and he read about this Blount's death in the newspaper. It seemed to disturb him, so much so that he couldn't finish his breakfast."

"Did he say what it was about Blount's death that upset him?"

"No, he tried to pretend that he wasn't upset, but I could see that he'd been thoroughly shaken. After he'd left for the office, I picked up the newspaper and read the piece on Craig Blount, but I couldn't find anything that warranted Robert's reaction."

"How long before his death was this?"

She laid the shears on the cement bench, as if they'd suddenly taken on weight. "Only about a week," she said. "That's why I remembered. Many things seemed to upset Robert during that period, but that newspaper story did particularly."

"May I use your telephone?" I asked her.

"Certainly. The door's unlocked." She bent gracefully to pick up the shears, to displace her grief again in the garden.

I phoned Alice Kramer, Manners' secretary, at Witlow Cable and asked her if she'd heard of Craig Blount. She hadn't, and she couldn't remember Manners' mentioning even a similar name in her presence.

I left Elizabeth Manners' home with an idea, about which I had more than a few doubts. But it was the only idea I had, so I clung to it.

At a large drugstore that sold everything from cough syrup to furniture, I got a handful of change from a schoolgirlish blonde cashier behind one of the registers and made my way to the phone booths.

The booths were in a secluded spot behind men's outerwear, and I was glad for the privacy. I fed change to the hungry telephone until it was glutted, then managed to get in touch with Dale Carlon.

"What have you learned?" Carlon asked immediately in his crisp business voice.

"I've got a connection between Talbert and Gratuity and the Robert Manners who killed himself, Manners and Gratuity and somebody named Craig Blount, who was killed in a hit-and-run accident in Seattle a few weeks ago."

"There is no Gratuity Insurance, Nudger. I checked."

"So did I. That's what interests me."

"Whoever or whatever they are, do you think my daughter is mixed up with them?"

137

"I'm reasonably sure of it."

Carlon's exasperated outlet of breath was amplified to a drawn-out rasping in the receiver. "You're keeping things quiet, aren't you, Nudger?"

"Too quiet. The police should know what I know, Mr. Carlon. If they did, you might see an extensive and effective investigation."

"We'll decide when and what to tell the police, Nudger."

What he meant by that was *he* would decide, and he had fifty thousand good arguments in his favor.

"Ever heard of *Business View?*" I asked him. "It's a magazine."

"I have. Used to subscribe to it."

"Then I take it it's a reputable publication."

"Very much so. I think it's published in Chicago. It's one of those financial monthlies that reports on the stock market and analyzes and predicts trends."

"There's a female reporter here who works for the magazine, gathering information about Manners' death. Her name's Alison Day."

"Alison?" He sounded surprised. "I know her well, Nudger. She's dedicated and, despite her comparative youth, widely respected in her profession. I've known Alison both professionally and as a friend of the family, for years. She recommended Joan to her college sorority."

"Then you vouch for her?"

"Completely. She's a thorough professional in her field. That's not to say, Nudger, that you should confide in her. She is a reporter."

"She doesn't know who I'm working for or why," I assured Carlon.

"I think you should go to Seattle," Carlon said after a pause.

"I don't think it's necessary at this point," I told him. "If I decide to, I'll let you know."

Gently I replaced the receiver, before he could insist. I had worked for Dale Carlons before; their egos demanded that they be better than everyone at everything.

On the way out of the drugstore, I stopped at the pharmaceutical counter and bought a fresh roll of antacid tablets. My next stop was going to be the Clairbank Hotel.

20

Alison's room at the Clairbank was large and comfortable. It lacked the careful color and style coordination of chain hotel rooms. The long triple dresser didn't quite match the smaller dresser on the opposite wall, two overstuffed wing chairs looked more like they belonged in an English men's club than a hotel room, and the flowered spread on the double bed matched neither beige carpet nor heavy drapes. The overall effect was one almost of hominess.

I could see a gleam in Alison's shrewd eyes as I told her what Craig Blount's name has evoked from Elizabeth Manners. Alison began to realize then, I think, that I was holding back a great deal from her.

"You're right about Gratuity Insurance," she said. "No such company is listed with—"

"I know," I told her, "it's been checked and double-checked."

She was wearing a tailored pinstriped outfit that couldn't subdue the curves of her lean body, and I found myself wondering if she would approach sex with her usual brisk and cool efficiency. The feline something in her eyes and the generous arc of her lower lip told me that wasn't likely.

"Where did you get the name of a fictitious insurance company?" she asked, pausing before the window in fetching silhouette.

"It's cropped up throughout my investigation. Now it's a link between Manners and Blount, two men who don't seem to be linked in any other way."

"Nudger," she said, "could you tell me what, precisely, you're investigating?"

I smiled and shook my head. "We agreed from the beginning there'd be some things I wouldn't tell you."

She narrowed an eye but didn't argue. "What do we do now?" she asked.

I was glad she said "we," because right now I needed her. "Can you draw up a list of the business establishment's top executives, nationwide?"

The suggestion didn't throw her. "How many names?"

"How about the top fifty? Not the obvious multimillionaires—the corporation men."

Alison walked to the writing desk, drummed longnailed fingers on smooth polished wood. "What do you intend to do with the list?"

"I want you to use your professional status to contact the secretaries or other satellite personalities who surround these men. Let them know that you want to be notified immediately if they hear of a Gratuity Insurance appointment. Can you do it?"

"Not as easily as you make it sound." She caressed her chin in thought. "How about my drawing up a list of the top people with whom I have connections, or with whose satellite personalities I have connections? I can't guarantee they'll be in the top fifty, but I feel safe to say they could all make the top hundred or two."

"That should help."

"And I can talk to the heads of some secretarial organizations," Alison said, picking up enthusiasm. "They can get the word out to their members to phone if they hear anything about Gratuity."

That was something I hadn't thought of, and it put the plan well into the realm of workability. "That's good," I told her. "The list doesn't have to read like a who's who. I want the names of executives in the same league as the men who died."

"Big league, but not the superstars," Alison said. She took a well-worn portable electric typewriter from the closet and set it on the desk. Then she dug through her luggage and came out with an expandable cardboard file and several flat leather-bound books. "This is going to take a long time," she said.

"Most everything worthwhile does," I told her sagely, myself doubting the wisdom of that pronouncement. "I'll look in on you later."

"Where are you going?"

"To see about some stocks."

As I closed the door behind me, I heard the ratchety sound of paper being rolled into the typewriter.

At the Gilford and Hollis brokerage firm, I talked to a broker's representative and got a prospectus on each of the five companies that had employed the dead executives whose names had been given to me by Alison, plus a prospectus on Witlow Cable.

I sat in a chair behind a low wooden railing, among several stricken-looking gentlemen who stared at the constantly sideways-traveling ribbon of the big board's lighted numerals, those numerals depicting the rise and fall of stock prices and men's fortunes in eighths of dollars. Now and then one of the men would seem to break the mesmeric spell of the lighted board, get up and walk over to check a teletype or speak in soft tones to one of the busy representatives at a row of desks beyond the railing. I was sure no one would disturb me as I settled back to examine the first prospectus, telling me in accountant's language all about a company called Avec-Stern.

A great deal of time, concentration and occasional help from one of the broker's representatives revealed no common denominator among the six companies for which the dead men had toiled. The main businesses of the companies were diverse: industrial cable, shoe manufacturing, heavy drilling equipment, bottling, trucking, and importing. Except for the bottling firm and heavy drilling equipment manufacturer, business was down the past several quarters for each company—at least on paper. And there had been no recent dramatic movement in the prices of their stocks. The broker's rep advised against my buying into any of them—except, possibly, the bottling firm.

Using a pay phone, I called Brian Cheevers and asked him if Witlow Cable had ever done business with any of the other companies. He promised to check, but his answer was a tentative no.

Outside the brokerage house I sat on a bench and tried to piece something together from what I'd learned inside. The weather was clear, and it wasn't so hot today. The sun felt good on my face and shoulders. I leaned back with my eyes half closed, watching through a haze the bright, multicolored stream of traffic, wondering if anything would ever fit together again for me.

Lornee was gone; and the children, gone, not just from me but from the world in which I lived. Life had taken a sudden, unpredictable direction, and now things seemed either too real or unreal, by turns. What was I doing here, on a curbside bench in Los Angeles, the sun on my face and a cold weight in my heart, full of fear and uncertainty as I goaded for greed the possibility of my violent death? What was anybody doing anywhere? I needed a drink.

But I knew better. I stood and moved away from the sun-warmed bench and the debilitating melancholy that I both courted and hated. As the traffic light changed and I crossed the concrete street in the sanctuary between parallel lines, I felt like an unreal man in an unreal city. The L.A. syndrome. This wasn't the place for me.

When I got back to the Clairbank, Alison had just finished telephoning, running up an enormous bill. I told her not to worry about the cost, that it came out of expenses.

"Maybe we can collect on it twice," she said, "me from my magazine and you from your client."

It occurred to me that I might want to sleep with her so I could reform her, but that didn't sound reasonable.

She leaned back from the phone, stiffly flexing the fingers of her right hand. Then she took her half-smoked cigarette from the ashtray, drew on it, and released thick smoke from her mouth sensuously, as if that were some exotic power she alone possessed and the cigarette had nothing to do with it.

"Getting cooperation?" I asked.

Alison laughed. "Of course. They're all afraid I'll write something nasty about their company and they'll lose their jobs."

"Did anyone you talked to know anything about Gratuity?"

"No. I thought they might, too. It would have saved us the trouble of waiting for a call."

"Maybe we won't have to wait long," I said. "Gratuity is pretty active for a nonexistent company." I tried not to show my disappointment at hearing that none of the people Alison had phoned knew anything about Gratuity. Maybe I expected too much. Interlocked and overlapping as the business world was, it was a vast world nonetheless.

Alison's telephone would have to be answerable at all times, so I offered to take a room at the Clairbank to spell her if she wanted to get out of the hotel. But she assured me that wasn't necessary, that she had volumes of work to do and would be glad to stay cooped up in her hotel room to do it while waiting for the phone call that might not come. Television would supply the entertainment; room service, the food.

I took a room at the Clairbank anyway.

During the next few days I got better acquainted with Alison, though not to the degree I had in mind. Maybe there was something to the "opposites attract" theory, because we seemed to hold opposite opinions on almost every subject. Or maybe Alison intrigued me because I didn't know how much of her was an act and how much was genuine. Sometimes she would say things in a certain tone, with a certain unguarded expression, and I would glimpse, beneath her surface, something like the fear that knotted my insides. Her facts and figures and cold logic, then, seemed a device to hold off a world that puzzled and frightened her.

On the third day, Alison's phone rang and I picked up the receiver. The call was from Chicago, and it was for Alison. I handed her the receiver and watched her cool and perfect features as she listened. As she replaced the receiver, she smiled a smile from one of those Italian Renaissance paintings.

"Somebody representing Gratuity Insurance has a nine o'clock appointment tomorrow morning in St. Louis with Tad Osborne, divisional manager of Heath Industries."

"What do you know about Osborne?"

"He's in his late forties, worked his way up through the sales division of Gayton Equipment, left them about five years ago to take over at Heath, an electronics component manufacturer with a lot of government contract work."

144

"How would you say Osborne ranks in the scheme of things with the six who died? In prestige, income, responsibility?"

Alison twisted a turquoise ring on her finger as she thought. "Generally they're in the same league, VIPs, but not the top men." She stood, looking at me expectantly, wondering, now, how we were going to act on the information we'd come up with.

"We should be able to get a flight to St. Louis today," I said.

"That's no problem," Alison said. "I have the airline schedules. The problem, as I see it, is getting Tad Osborne's cooperation."

"Leave that to me," I told her with some pleasure, watching her cock her head with inquisitive surprise.

Alison's lips parted, and I thought she was going to ask me how I was going to handle Osborne, but she said, "I'll get reservations on the next available flight."

We had two hours until flight time. I left Alison to her packing and went to my room and phoned Dale Carlon.

21

Los Angeles had been hot, but St. Louis had it beat. This was the damp, sticky kind of heat that followed you indoors, made you perspire even when you were still, and melted the body from the fabric of your clothes so that they clung limply to you.

I waited for our luggage to come around on the metal

carousel while Alison made her way through the milling throng of travelers and greeters to rent a car. A woman rattled off flight numbers over the public address speakers as if she were calling a bingo game. No one seemed to be listening.

Our luggage came up fast, and Alison was just completing arrangements for the car when I met her at the Avis desk. The terminal's cocktail lounge looked dim and cool as we walked past, and I could have used a drink but thought better of it. It was almost midnight, and tomorrow morning I might have to be sharper than I'd ever been.

Alison drove the rented Chevy too fast to the Ramada Inn near the airport. We took adjoining rooms, an unnecessary expense in my estimation but not in hers.

I stretched out on the bed and expected to lie awake for a long time, but when I blinked, it was seven A.M. and time to get moving to make Heath Industries before nine. A cold shower focused my mind on my fear, and I dressed more slowly than I should have. But nothing I did slowed the minute hand on my watch.

Alison was downstairs, waiting for me. We had a quick breakfast of Danish rolls and coffee, then walked out onto the already-warm blacktopped parking lot and got into the rented Chevy. I drove, knowing I'd be less nervous if I kept myself occupied.

Heath Industries was in Westport, a new and sprawling industrial development, west of the city, that was either the downtown or the slum of the future. The morning rush hour traffic was a study in heat and frustration, and it was eight-thirty when we finally parked in the lot of Heath's regional headquarters in an impressive, recently built, tall structure fronted by an artificial lake from which rose a graceful, gull-winged cement sculpture. The Heath building was the tallest in the area and commanded a view of a teeming four-lane highway that dwindled to a sun-shimmering ribbon on the horizon.

146

We topped the cement steps and entered the lobby—high-ceilinged, decorous and cool. A gold-framed directory told us that Tad Osborne's office was on the top floor. The elevator was a smooth rocket that didn't help my stomach.

A blond Nordic type with too much bulky jewelry sat at a desk in the plush outer office. She smiled at us when we entered and told her who we were, and she seemed to know Alison. Osborne must have instructed her to send us right in when she buzzed him, because she immediately jangled over to the main office and opened the door for us.

Tad Osborne's office was cool and ordered, and beyond a huge window the ribbon of teeming highway stretched to an even more distant horizon. Osborne himself was a medium-sized, balding man with broad, pleasant features, seated behind a very wide desk on which sat only the basics—pen set, ashtray, "out" basket, telephone, and on one corner the mandatory framed family photographs.

"What is it about Mr. Bender that interests you?" Osborne asked after we'd been seated.

Alison arched an eyebrow beautifully. "Mr. Bender?"

"Why, yes . . . Frank Bender, the Gratuity Insurance agent."

"There's really not much we can tell you, Mr. Osborne," I said, "because we don't have hard information. Why did Bender want to see you?"

Osborne rotated back and forth slightly in his swivel chair, but his gray eyes stayed trained on me. "He called and said there'd been a series of insurance company mergers and he needed my signature to transfer some of my policies. He assured me it would mean a savings without loss of coverage."

"Whatever he tells you, Mr. Osborne, I'm afraid you're on your own. We don't know enough to predict exactly what he'll really have in mind, but there's sufficient reason for us to believe it won't be insurance."

"I'm sure there is, or Dale Carlon wouldn't have vouched for you." He looked at his digital watch. "It's quarter to nine. How is this thing going to unfold?"

I didn't tell him that that question was ruining my health. "Just pretend we're not here. Listen to what Bender has to say, tell him what you think best, and when he leaves, I'll follow him. If it's all right, I'll wait in the file room off your secretary's office so I can see him enter and leave."

"Fine," Osborne said. "I'll tell Mary to cooperate with you."

"Miss Day will be waiting with me, and when I've left she'll want to talk to you to get all the details of your conversation with Bender while they're fresh in your mind."

"Suppose I record our conversation without his knowledge?"

"I wouldn't advise it. Bender might have one of a number of devices to detect an operating recorder."

"Our talk should only take a few minutes," Alison said through her best interviewer's smile. "I'm with *Business View*, but I promise you nothing you tell me will be used without your permission."

I thought she was putting herself in a corner there, but I kept quiet.

"I've read some of your articles with interest, Miss Day," Osborne said, spreading thick honey. "You do fine and accurate work."

"Bender should be arriving any time now," I told him. "It would be better if he didn't see us."

Osborne rose and showed us out of his office, resting a hand on Alison's shoulder in what I assumed to be a fatherly manner. A favorable article in *Business View* wouldn't hurt either Heath Industries or his career.

The file room was almost as large as the anteroom. It was furnished with two wooden chairs, a table, and three walls lined solid with charcoal-gray file cabinets. The fourth wall was all metal shelving stacked with varied but neatly stored office supplies. Alison took a chair near the table. I propped the file room door open at just the right angle and positioned the remaining chair so I had a view of anyone entering the outer office and approaching Osborne's bejeweled secretary.

My nerves took over, tapping my right toe in staccato rhythm on the cork floor, rubbing the fingertips of my right hand on the tabletop until they tingled.

But I didn't have long to wait. Five minutes after I'd sat down, at exactly nine o'clock, Frank Bender arrived.

He was a well-groomed and stylishly dressed man in his late twenties or early thirties, wearing a neat dark suit that went far to disguise the fact that he was overweight. He had an even-featured, handsome face with bright, small dark eyes narrowed by the fleshy padding around them. Holding his attaché case before him, he aimed exactly the right sort of friendly but impersonal smile at the secretary, and I heard him small-talking her as he gave his name.

Osborne's secretary seemed genuinely charmed as she got up and ushered Bender into the main office. She was still smiling at something he'd said as she walked back toward her desk.

Alison and I looked at each other. There was an anxious, super-alert expression in her eyes, and I wondered if I wore the same expression.

No, I was sure mine was tempered by worry and fear. The things that could go wrong! Might Gratuity be legitimate, a small or newly formed company not yet brought to the attention of the various agencies that had been contacted? Frank Bender looked like a thousand other insurance agents, didn't he?

Then I thought about the business card in Victor Talbert's jacket, in Chicago, on the back of which was the name of a man who'd died a violent death in Los Angeles. As Victor Talbert had died. As Craig Blount, in Seattle, had died.

It was nine-twenty, and Bender hadn't come out. My stomach was vibrating.

He came out at nine twenty-eight, and by then I was on my feet, waiting. Through the crack in the door I saw him walk past Osborne's secretary and smile as he did when he entered. He said something I couldn't understand as he went out, and the secretary smiled and adjusted an earring. With a last look back at Alison, who was now also standing, I left the file room to follow Bender.

He left the parking lot in a light-tan sedan, probably a rental, and I trailed in the Avis Chevy. He wound his way through the streets almost as if he didn't know exactly where he was. I stayed three cars back, eating antacid tablets like candy.

Bender must have skipped breakfast. I watched him pull up to a hamburger restaurant, one of a chain, that had a sign proclaiming that they served eggs and pancakes. Parked in an inconspicuous spot near a discount store, I waited for him and thought of things other than food.

I hadn't carried a gun since I was with the department, and I wondered if I should have one now. Bender looked harmless enough, even amiable, but I remembered the deceptively peaceful death photos of Victor Talbert and the fear on Belle Dee's bloodied face when she opened her apartment door for me. And I remembered my own reaction to the sight of her injuries.

Bender finally emerged from the restaurant, his suit coat unbuttoned and his stocky arms swinging freely, the expansive walk of a well-fed man. I watched him get into his car; then I saw a hazy rush of exhaust

150

fumes from the tailpipe of the tan sedan, and it backed from its parking slot and maneuvered in tight quarters to point toward the driveway to the street.

I started the Chevy and sat with the engine idling. When Bender turned the sedan into the flow of traffic, I reminded myself of Carlon's fifty thousand dollars and followed.

Bender was driving more confidently now, as if he knew where he was going. He was easier to follow.

We took a cloverleaf and were on Highway 67, where it was called Lindbergh Boulevard. Within a few minutes Bender made a left into the parking lot of the King Saint Louis Motel.

The motel was small and not very prosperous-looking, a series of duplex cabins. Bender must already have registered. The tan car made a sharp turn and parked in front of the end cabin. I watched as Bender got out of the car, carrying his attaché case, and let himself into the cabin through the door nearest me.

I sat in the car, parked on the gravel road shoulder off Lindbergh, and looked at the cabin's closed door. With a shattering roar, a jet passed almost directly overhead, so low it seemed the treetops flinched. The King Saint Louis was one of a string of motels directly west of the airport. I eased the Chevy forward, turned into the parking lot and, with a soft squeal of brakes, stopped in front of the tiny office.

I asked for one of the cabins nearest the highway. There were plenty of vacancies, as the sparse-haired elderly woman behind the desk informed me, and she was more than glad to comply. I registered under my own name and paid in advance.

The cabins were strung unevenly along a line diagonal to the highway. From my front window I could see Bender's parked car and the front of his cabin. All of the cabins were in minor disrepair, faded redwood with patchwork shingled roofs. I could see tall weeds beyond the back corners of most of them, and outside the window of the back door of my own.

The telephone had a long cord, just long enough to reach the table by the front window. I set the phone down, moved a lamp aside and pulled a wicker-backed chair next to the table. Never letting the front of Bender's cabin out of my sight for more than a few seconds, I dialed the number of Heath Industries and asked for Tad Osborne.

There was something in the voice of the girl who answered the phone as she asked me again whom I was calling, then requested me to hold the line—a high edge of excitement. The next voice I heard was a man's, but not Osborne's.

"Who's calling, please?"

I started to speak, but an uneasiness, a subtle tingling of suspicion, bored into my mind.

"Hello, who's—"

I replaced the receiver.

For a long while I sat still, staring out through the dusty, slanted venetian blinds at the quiet, sun-brightened face of Bender's cabin. Maybe the girl on the phone at Heath had some personal reason to be excited. Maybe she'd given me the wrong extension and the man's voice was simply that of another Heath employee. Maybe nothing was wrong. Maybe it was.

I phoned Heath Industries again, got the same girl, then the same laconic male voice asking me to identify myself. Not office procedure—police procedure.

I punched the button in the telephone's cradle, dialed the Ramada Inn and asked for Alison's room.

No answer.

I hung up the phone and sat staring out the window. Another jet roared overhead, sending vibrations through the flimsy cabin. I had no way of knowing what, if anything, had gone wrong at Heath, or where

152

Alison was, or if Bender had somehow been tipped to my presence. Doggedly I told myself things might actually be going smoothly—nothing wrong at Heath, and Alison hadn't had time to return to the Ramada, where she was supposed to wait for my phone call. But the fear lay like a slab of lead in my stomach, and my chest seemed to be constricting my heart.

I was plagued by the feeling that events had passed from my control, that the tiger I'd had by the tail had finally turned around. But there was nothing I could do about it now; I could only go on with what I'd planned. I'd try the Ramada again in a while, talk to Alison and get some of the answers.

Noon arrived, passed, and Alison still hadn't returned to her motel room. And Bender's cabin—half in shadow now, peaceful, drapes closed—might have been vacant but for the fact that I knew he was inside. The tan sedan was parked, unmoved and baking in the sun, where Bender had left it.

My back began to ache, and I got up now and then to pace, occasionally sitting down to make another unsuccessful phone call to the Ramada. The intermittent overhead roar of jet engines was beginning to wear on me.

Then, at two o'clock, the door to Bender's cabin opened and he came out.

He'd changed clothes. Now he was wearing gray slacks and a pale-yellow sport shirt. Maybe he'd been asleep; he looked fresh. I stood at the window, leaning over the table and watching him.

I cursed silently as Bender walked past his parked car. At first I thought he was going to the motel office, but instead he turned left and stood on the shoulder of the highway, leaning forward, waiting to cross.

When there was a break in the traffic, he trotted across the highway, and I watched him walk south on the other side. I realized then where he was going. The

King Saint Louis didn't have a restaurant, and Bender was headed for the restaurant of the motel across the street for a late lunch.

I had to move to the side, hold back the drapes and peer at an angle through the window now to follow his progress. He passed out of my sight momentarily, but I picked him up again as he entered the motel restaurant. I relaxed my grip on the drapes and stepped back. My stomach said no to what I had to do next.

Walking to the back door of my cabin, I examined the lock. Simple, the sort that can be slipped with a piece of celluloid or a plastic credit card. But there was also a chain lock. I could only hope that the back door of Bender's cabin didn't have one; or, if it did, that it wasn't fastened. Parting the stained sheer curtains over the window in my door, I took a quick look out back, saw only tall weeds and a small gray trash container, and stepped outside.

Slipping the lock on the rear of Bender's cabin was no problem, but the door did have a chain lock and it was fastened. I saw what I'd have to do. If I punched out the door's small windowpane nearest the lock and cleaned up the broken glass, Bender would never know it unless he happened to look behind the door's curtains. My heart was pumping with labored wildness and my body was bent by the tightness in my stomach. I wondered how professional burglars ever got up the nerve to operate. With a fast, guilty look around, I rammed my elbow into the window, and the glass broke in four pieces but didn't fall from the frame. No damage to my elbow, and I was grateful there hadn't been much noise.

I removed the largest piece of glass, reached in and, with fumbling fingers, unfastened the chain. Then I added breaking and entering to withholding evidence and went inside.

It was almost as if I'd found shelter; I couldn't be

seen now. But the exhilaration and fear had entered with me. I could hear the sounds of my own breathing and rushing of blood, and only my rising anger with myself brought a measure of calm.

The interior of Bender's cabin was exactly like mine. A suitcase stood open on a luggage stand at the foot of the double bed, revealing folded white underwear and shirts. Bender's leather attaché case was on the floor, leaning against the side of the dresser. I went to it first, found it unlocked.

The case was empty but for a gold letter-opener and a thin packet of white business cards. The cards were similar to the card I'd found in the pocket of Victor Talbert's jacket, engraved only with GRATUITY INSURANCE.

I closed the attaché case and leaned it back the way I'd found it. Then I went to the suitcase and searched carefully beneath the folded clothes. It took me a while, and I found nothing but lint.

After rearranging the suitcase the way it had been, I checked the bathroom. Nothing there but a zippered travel kit containing the usual assortment of shaving cream, razor, spray deodorant and manicure set.

From the bathroom I went quickly to the closet. I'd been inside Bender's cabin for little more than five minutes, and I told myself it would be safer to slow down and do things right than to panic. He probably wouldn't return for at least half an hour.

The closet contained a suit, a sport coat and two pale-blue shirts on hangers. A search of the pockets netted me nothing but a postage stamp and comb. I straightened the shirts on their hangers, smoothed the lapels of the suit.

The blast of a jet engine made me take a step toward the back door; then I stood leaning on the dresser, waiting for the sound to subside.

In the first dresser drawer I opened I found a dollar's

worth of change and a set of gold cufflinks. The rest of the drawers were empty.

I stood in the center of the cabin and looked desperately around. There was nowhere else to search. I'd risked everything for nothing.

After making sure things were arranged the way I'd found them, I moved toward the back door. And that's when I saw the strip of white beneath the dark suitcase.

I stepped over, lifted the end of the suitcase and discovered that what I'd seen was the edge of an airline ticket. It was made out to Emmett Marshal, either Bender's real name or the name he traveled under, and it was a return-flight ticket to Chicago. The departure time was noon tomorrow. I replaced the ticket where I'd found it, letting the edge of white show as it had before.

When I left Bender's cabin, I removed the remaining broken glass from the back door's window frame and made sure the curtains hung completely over the opening. I dropped the pieces of broken glass onto some soggy cardboard in the gray trash container as I passed, and I entered my own cabin the back way and locked the door behind me.

The floor seemed to be made of sponge. I sat weakly on the edge of the bed and realized that I was practically panting, winded from doing nothing more than holding my breath.

After a few minutes I involuntarily laughed out loud, and that seemed to drain me of my tension. I got up, crossed to the telephone and dialed the number of the Ramada Inn, knowing it well enough now to dial it without thinking. When I asked for Alison's room, her telephone was answered on the first ring.

There was anxiety and weariness in Alison's voice instead of the usual crispness.

I sat down in my chair by the front window. "Alison, where were you earlier?"

"Talking to the police."

"The police? . . ." My fingers were suddenly slippery with perspiration on the smooth receiver.

"Tad Osborne's been murdered."

Fear rushed into me. I didn't know whether to curse my bad luck or my stupidity.

That I should curse my greed never occurred to me.

22

Twenty minutes after leaving the King Saint Louis Motel, I entered Alison's room at the Ramada Inn.

She was on the phone, her lips compressed in exasperation. When she spoke, it was with the brittle self-control of someone who'd rather be screaming. "I will," she said, "you can count on it."

When she hung up the phone, she sighed. "My editor," she explained. "He thinks I'm on another assignment and I have to stall him."

The police must have been thorough with her. She wasn't her usual composed self. Some of the shrewd confidence was gone from her eyes, and a stray wisp of auburn hair hung over the center of her forehead.

"How did it happen?" I asked her.

Alison brushed back the strand of hair and paced off some of her nervousness. "After you left to follow Bender I went into Osborne's office to talk to him. He was sitting with his head resting on his desk, his eyes open, as if he were looking toward the door. . . ." Her face was pale wax.

"Only he was dead," I finished for her.

Alison nodded, swallowed. The strain was pulling at the corners of her mouth.

"How?" I asked her.

"He was . . . stabbed, in the chest."

An iciness dropped through me as I remembered the gold letter-opener in Bender's attaché case.

"Did the police find the weapon?"

"No, the killer took it with him."

"Bender. . . . " I said.

Alison gave me an intent look. "It had to be him, but the police don't know who or where he is."

I could imagine Osborne's mistake. He knew we were onto Bender and reasoned that he was in no danger, so he must have pushed too hard, maybe lost his temper, underestimating the ruthlessness and deadliness of Bender and whatever he represented.

"Did you tell the police I was following Bender?"

"Not right away," Alison said, "but I had to eventually. I told them what I knew."

I walked to the window with my fists in my pockets. If I told the police where to find Bender, they'd pick him up and, with that, end my hopes of tracing Joan Clark. I was certain that she was somehow connected with Gratuity Insurance.

"Suppose that Bender realized I was following him, and that he lost me," I said.

"But he didn't."

"From this point on we pretend that I told you he did."

Alison gave me a nice eyebrow arch. "But you can't withhold evidence in a murder case."

I didn't tell her she was too late with that advice or that Carlon was paying me fifty thousand dollars to follow his advice.

"We're too close not to," I told her. "I searched Bender's motel room while he was out. He's going to be on flight five sixty-two tomorrow at noon, bound for Chicago, which is where he came from."

158

Alison appeared dubious. She touched the flame of her lighter to one of her long cigarettes and glared at me through the smoke. "Nudger, what have you got in mind?"

"I intend to take an earlier flight to Chicago. I'll be at O'Hare when Bender's plane touches down, and I'll follow him from the airport."

"To where?"

"That's what I'll be following him to find out."

I watched Alison take another desperate drag on her cigarette, glad I hadn't confided in her completely. She seemed to relax, letting the smoke filter thickly from her mouth and nostrils.

"What if Bender changes his flight plan?" she asked.

"The Benders of the world don't change their carefully laid-out plans unless they have to. You can bet that killing Osborne was in Bender's mind as an alternative before he walked into that office. And now he knows that if he ever does come under suspicion, it would be best if he left a record of having behaved normally after leaving Heath Industries. Remember, he doesn't know he was followed."

Alison stared at her cigarette and seemed to weigh the logic of what I'd told her. "I'll go to Chicago with you," she said.

"It might only implicate you further."

"I'm not implicated at all yet."

The message was communicated clearly. If I didn't let her accompany me, what was there left for her to do but cover herself by telling the police what she knew?"

"You *are* asking me to break the law," Alison said. "And remember, I'm the one who steered you onto Bender. We agreed to help each other with an exchange of information, so don't expect me to back away from this story now."

"I don't want you complicating things. I don't want anyone else to get hurt."

"And I want my story."

I knew I had no choice, really. If Alison called the police, I'd never be able to leave St. Louis, and I'd be in hot water a mile over my head.

"All right, but there's a condition," I told her, pretending to have a few bargaining chips. "I'll be in charge in Chicago, without any interference from you for the sake of a good story."

"If it will help your ego," she said.

I told her to make the reservations.

23

At eleven thirty the next morning I was in Chicago, sitting behind a bourbon and water in the airport lounge, waiting for the minute hand to make another circuit. Alison and I had arrived on the ten-twenty flight from St. Louis. She had gone to check in with her magazine, and I'd instructed her to meet me later in the day at the TraveLodge, on South Michigan Avenue. I'd already rented a car and had my luggage in the trunk. Bender's flight wasn't due to arrive until twelve thirty-two. It was waiting and thinking time.

Alison was the subject of my thoughts as I sat waiting for the liquor to calm me, to numb some of the fear in me. There was fear, but not to the degree that I'd be careless. A thin line there, increasingly hard to discern.

What was there about Alison? What inconsistency was stirring, invisible in the back of my mind? She ever threatened to become a dilemma in the case, and yet it was she who had gotten me this far.

And though I'd pursued the investigation in the only direction I'd seen open to me, would it actually lead to Joan Clark? Collecting the remainder of my fifty thousand dollars depended on that alone. Again I experienced that foreboding, that gradually heightening perception of a drawing nearer, an inexorable movement toward the vortex.

What if Alison was right about the possibility of Bender's having changed flights? It wasn't likely, but unlikely things happened all the time, and to me. Where would I be if he had changed flights, slipped away?

I knew where. I downed the rest of the drink I'd intended to nurse.

At twelve thirty-five I watched Frank Bender pass through security, wondering if he still had the gold letter-opener or if he'd disposed of it in St. Louis.

Weighted down as he was with his luggage, it was simple to follow him through the crowded terminal. But he did what I'd hoped he wouldn't and headed toward the taxi area.

Things got less simple then. I had to run to where my car was parked, and the damned thing refused to start. On the fourth try, when the starter was growling like a record played at slow speed, the engine turned over and I gunned it in frustration before jamming the shift lever into drive. Luck was the big reason I was able to get behind Bender's cab as it turned onto the expressway and headed for the city.

Inside the city limits the cab turned right onto Fifty, drove awhile, then made a left and began to wind through side streets. I followed well back in the light midday traffic. The cab had a mud-splotched liquor advertisement on its trunk and a limber whip antenna, and that made keeping track of it easy.

We passed through an old and doomed area of the city, then on into a marginal neighborhood of small shops and brick apartment buildings, and suddenly things began to look familiar.

The cab veered to the curb and parked beneath a block-lettered sign: EXECUTIVE TOWERS. I looked at the recently face-lifted apartment building as I drove past. Jerry Congram's former home.

Parked down the street, I watched in my rearview mirror as Frank Bender got out of the cab with his luggage and entered the building. The taxi's battered grill moved to the left in my mirror, and I turned off my engine as the cab shot past me with its backseat unoccupied.

I kept an eye on the building entrance in my mirror for about ten minutes, then I got out of the car and walked back along the sidewalk.

There was no Frank Bender on the Executive Towers' mailboxes, no Emmett Marshal. Bender must have been living here under a third name. I considered asking the manager about him, but that might only serve to tip Bender. One thing I could be fairly sure of was that, after leaving owing three months' rent, Jerry Congram hadn't moved back into the Executive Towers. I crossed the red and white tile floor, left the lobby and walked back to my car.

I passed the time by sitting in the rental car and then in a booth in a little doughnut shop across the street, waiting for Bender to emerge from the apartment building. This was the endless, monotonous part of my job. The disc jockeys on the car radio began telling the same jokes, playing the same music; the coffee tasted like the cup before, only worse, leaving a bitter aftertaste and frayed nerves; and the pavement I occasionally walked along to loosen my leg muscles became a treadmill.

The sun was setting, angling long dark shadows and softening the sharp vertical edges of the buildings. Supper was two glazed doughnuts washed down with more black coffee.

When the sky was almost completely dark and I was sitting behind the wheel of the rented Chevy, enjoying the breeze between the rolled-down windows, Bender walked out of the Executive Towers. He was wearing a dark business suit and carrying his attaché case and a precautionary light raincoat.

I sat up straight, started the engine and let it idle. Bender walked to a small green sports car, a convertible with its canvas top up. He unlocked the car, tossed the attaché case and folded coat inside, then lowered himself into the front seat. The sports car jumped forward and edged into the sparse traffic, and with a gentle touch on the accelerator I followed the low red taillights.

We took side streets for a while, then got onto Fifty but soon made a left onto a wide street with a grassy median. Traffic began to thin out as we drove for almost half an hour, then the median disappeared. Soon we were in a suburbia of middle-class tract houses and strip shopping centers. The sports car led me left on another narrow road, and the subdivision houses were fewer and farther apart.

Brake lights flared red ahead of me, and I slowed and watched Bender make a right turn. When I reached where he'd turned, I saw an unmarked dark road leading up a rise. I got a glimpse of twin taillights as the sports car took the rise toward some distant yellow lights, then I drove past the unmarked intersection to a spot where the road shoulder was wide and I could turn around.

When I reached the steep side road I sat for a while. My stomach was quivering, not helped by all the bitter coffee I'd drunk, and my heart was hammering out a warning. But I'd come this far. And, dammit, it was a public road. I jerked the wheel to the left and accelerated.

The narrow road was blacktopped but in need of repair. Deep chuckholes rocked the car every five or ten seconds as I drove steadily uphill. I passed a small, faded wooden billboard that told me I was driving toward Devon Acres, a subdivision of "affordable luxury."

The road flattened out, flanked by woods. I rounded a curve, and scattered over a wide stretch of flat land was Devon Acres.

Most of the lots were empty, though there were a few houses under construction. The houses that were fully built and spaced widely over the area were all lighted. Judging by the faded sign I'd seen, Devon Acres was one of those big subdivisions that had started strong but fallen into financial difficulty. I spotted the low-slung taillights of Bender's car far ahead of me, saw them merge as the car slowed and turned. Then I watched the play of his headlights flash behind large trees as he went up what appeared to be a driveway to the most isolated of the long ranch houses.

I drove past without slowing, quickly studying the house. Lights were burning in the west side, and it was built as at the base of a wooded hill. There were several other cars parked about the house and in the long driveway.

If I could park in an unnoticeable spot, I could cut around to the back of the house through the trees. There wasn't more than a dozen or so houses occupied in Devon Acres, so the risk of being spotted by a neighbor was small. It was a workable plan, I knew. The question was, did I have the guts. The answer was no, but I had the need.

The street curved slightly, and I parked the car in the drive of a partially built house, where it was invisible from the house Bender had entered. I got out without slamming the car door and walked quickly into the darkness at the side of the skeletal-roofed house.

For a while I stood bent over with my hands on my knees. Fear was making me sick. In a few minutes the sickness passed, but not the fear, and I entered the woods.

I didn't understand how anyone could move silently through the woods at night. Every step I took seemed to bring an explosion of crashing brush and splintering twigs. I told myself that the noise seemed louder than it was, that I was right on top of it. But I wasn't very convincing.

Suddenly the square light of a window appeared through the trees, no more than fifteen feet from me. I had been dropping downhill without realizing it as I moved toward the house. My right hand shot out to brace myself against a tree, then scraped rough bark soundlessly as I lowered myself to a squatting position. This was closer than I'd intended to get, but here I was.

I was looking into a bedroom that seemed unoccupied. The floor was bare wood, and I could see a made bed and the corner of a dresser. The walls were white, freshly painted and free of decorations.

Keeping low and backing a few feet into the cover of the woods, I moved to my left and the next lighted window. This window had drapes, but they were partly open. I saw a dim shadow movement inside, and I inched farther to my left and closer so I could see into the room.

There was Bender, standing at the end of a long polished wood table. His attaché case was open on the table and he was reading from a sheet of white paper, glancing up now and then to gauge the effect of his words on his audience.

That audience was five men and at least three women seated at the long table in the otherwise unfurnished room. They were all neatly dressed, sitting erect and listening intently to whatever Bender was saying. At the head of the table sat a man in his late twenties, almost foppishly well dressed, wavy dark hair in a short but stylish cut, keen blue eyes. He seemed to be in charge, and occasionally he'd interrupt Bender to ask a question, then jot notes in an open file before him. I knew I was looking at Jerry Congram.

Maybe Bender was reporting that he'd had to kill Tad Osborne. I saw a marked reaction around the table, bodies leaning back, hands in motion on the polished wood, heads turning slightly to check other responses. Congram was sitting perfectly still, with absolute calm. He rapped on the table a few times with the cap of his pen.

All eyes were focused again on Bender, and he began to read. Congram seemed to be taking more notes.

What I knew I should do was exactly what I wanted to do: get away with what information I had.

When I stood to back away from the window, my left leg was asleep, and I lurched slightly. A dead branch I hadn't realized was against my shoulder cracked and fell loudly to the ground.

Almost immediately a face was at the window, suspicious, angry. I was crouched again, motionless, as the man peered out into the darkness. I watched his eyes roam, seeking an object on which to fix themselves. The expression on his intent face remained the same as his gaze passed over me twice. At the slightest indication that he'd seen me I was ready to run for my car. My legs were even more ready than I was, and my heart was pumping as if I were already running.

After a final dart-eyed look around, the man turned, said something.

The lights in the room went out.

The man could see outside more clearly now, without the reflections on the window. I almost straightened and bolted. I could barely make him out through the dark glass, the same angry expression on his face, as if he wanted to find someone. More faces appeared at the window. At least I was wearing dark clothing,

166

and I was almost completely concealed by some sort of viny plant. Their eyes still weren't accustomed to the dark, and I knew if I had the nerve to stay still I probably wouldn't be seen. I was glad the window was closed; they might have smelled my fear.

Then suddenly the lights came back on, the drapes swished closed. The house's occupants seemed to have decided the noise they'd heard was of nonhuman origin.

I remained where I was, without moving, for another few minutes, fighting my powerful urge to break and run, willing my tensed muscles to relax.

Then, very slowly, with the greatest of care, I moved directly away from the house. When I thought I'd moved far enough up the hill, I began making my way through the trees in the direction of my parked car. I walked faster as I put distance between myself and the house, putting more of a premium on speed than on silence with each step. The woods were thinner now. Low brush snapped and swished at my ankles, and I no longer had to constantly brush branches away from my face in the darkness. I was already squeezing the car's ignition key in my right hand, though I couldn't recall reaching into my pocket for it.

I got to the car, managed to open the door with a fear-awkward hand and clambered in behind the steering wheel. I was careful to close the door without slamming it. On the second try I hit the keyhole with the ignition key and thanked assorted gods as the engine turned over. After backing from the driveway, I forced myself to drive slowly—simply someone passing through the subdivision who had innocent reason to be there. I knew now that I'd make it if no one heard my heart.

The car bucked as it took the steep, chuckholed road, then seemed to be grateful for smooth road as I made a left turn and drove for the city.

What I had witnessed, I realized, was a Gratuity Insurance business meeting, and the topic of business was Tad Osborne's murder. No doubt it had been Gratuity "agents" who'd beaten Belle Dee, trying to erase a link between the murdered Victor Talbert and the company. To have killed her, too, might only have triggered a deeper, more dangerous investigation.

And how much did Gratuity know about me? Was it my presence at the Poptop Club and at Belle Dee's apartment that had prompted her beating? I wished I knew more about Gratuity Insurance and Jerry Congram. I understood enough now to be really scared, maybe enough on which to act.

Bender, at least, would be a sure-fire suspect for Osborne's murder, and he could probably be made to talk in the process of plea bargaining. I thought about Osborne and the shock it must have been for him to realize his fatal mistake. Maybe he'd gone further with Bender than he would have, to impress Alison.

Then I remembered something about the conversation in Osborne's office, and dominoes began to fall.

When I reached the city, it occurred to me that I might actually have been spotted back at Devon Acres and that someone might be following me. For about fifteen minutes I drove aimless patterns on bleak side streets, breaking traffic laws a few times to see if anyone would break them with me rather than be left behind.

By the time I was satisfied that I wasn't being followed, I was lost. But my pulse was comfortably slower. I was about to stop and consult my street map when I found myself on Fifty once again and regained my sense of direction.

When I registered at the TraveLodge, they told me at the desk that Alison had left a message. She would be waiting for me in the cocktail lounge until ten. The wall clock behind the desk read nine fifteen. I thanked

168

the clerk, and he told me where the lounge was and gave me a room key.

I entered the dim, quiet lounge and walked to where Alison was sitting, sipping a tall, clear drink. Her eyes widened slightly as she looked up at me, and I smiled at her and sat down.

"Where have you been?" she asked, somewhat in the tone of an irate wife.

"To a place called Devon Acres, one of those partially constructed subdivisions with more hope than houses."

"You look like you had some trouble."

For the first time I realized the evening's activities had taken a toll on my appearance. My hands were dirty and scratched and there was a small, jagged tear in the right sleeve of my sport coat. My hair was mussed, and no doubt there was grime on my face.

I ordered a double bourbon on the rocks and told Alison everything that had happened.

When I finished, she sat surveying me with a look of narrow-eyed intelligence, a white curve of smoke drifting like an ethereal question mark above her cigarette in the ashtray at her elbow. "Now are you going to the police?"

"Yes," I said, "but not right away like I should. First I'm going to claim the right that I've earned to nail down my end of this business. I think it's time for you to take me to Joan Clark."

The surprise passed from her face in an instant, but an instant was all I needed. I knew Alison was too smart to deny knowing Joan Clark's whereabouts.

She picked the cigarette from the ashtray, absently replaced it without drawing on it. Now that I was bringing the police in on the case, Alison had little choice but to do as I asked.

"Joan's in my apartment," she flatly admitted. "How did you guess I was hiding her?"

"Dale Carlon mentioned that you were a family friend," I said, "and that you knew Joan. Where would Joan go for help in her predicament, afraid for her life? Not to the police or to her father. Not to a private investigator, one of a bad type and a total stranger. But you, a family friend, another woman and a trained investigator in your work, could understand and have a professional interest. And more importantly, you could work on the case without attracting suspicion. You could arrange for the arrest of the people who wanted to kill her, and maybe she thought she could stay out of it."

Alison toyed with her tall glass, nodded. "At first she thought that, then she wanted me to find Congram so she could try to buy her life with her father's money. Joan has faith in me. I was sort of her big sister–godmother when she was younger."

"Does Carlon know where she is?"

Alison snubbed out her cigarette with short jabs. "No, Joan never talked to him. The seriousness of her situation dawned on her by degrees. Now she realizes money can't guarantee her safety. She simply wants her potential killers off her trail, in the hands of the law. I thought she was safe with me; I guess I made some mistakes."

"Not many," I said. "I knew someone was touching bases before me at times and thought it was whoever had killed Talbert, but it was you, working the same trail I was. I was searching for Joan Clark and you were working for her, searching for Congram. When you got the call about Osborne, it came from Chicago; I figured that for some reason you'd routed some of the calls through your office. But yesterday you were on the phone with your editor, conning him into thinking you were chasing another story. You'd already had feelers out for a Gratuity Insurance appointment, to be called to your home number, where Joan would always be waiting to forward the message to you. It was Joan who phoned from Chicago about the Osborne appointment."

Alison played her lighter flame over the tip of another of her long cigarettes, leaned back. I enjoyed the frank admiration in her green cat eyes. "You pieced things together neatly, Nudger, I'll admit. What about Osborne's remark in his office?"

"Now who needs ego boosting?" I asked her. "I knew you were too sharp not to have noticed when Osborne mentioned that Dale Carlon had arranged the appointment for us, but what he said didn't register with me until later. I never told you who'd hired me, and you let Osborne's remark go by without question. Not like you at all, Alison."

She'd wanted to hear that last part. She smiled at me.

"I think we should go," I said, and she agreed with me.

24

Alison's apartment wasn't the worst place to hide. It was on the seventh floor, and large, filled with modern furniture that somehow managed to appear comfortable. The pale walls were graced with multicolored inkblot paintings that seemed to be there more for the brown and yellow color scheme than for art. Two wide glass doors led to a garden balcony, the ledges of which were lined with narrow planters of tangled green vines.

Alison looked around, glanced at me as if surprised not to see Joan Clark in the apartment. Then she walked to a closed door and knocked on it.

"Joan? It's me, Alison. You can come out."

Alison was about to knock again when the door opened slowly and Joan Clark stepped out.

When she saw me, her slender body gave a slight backward jerk, and her large dark eyes darted sideways to question Alison mutely. She was wearing a wrinkled gray pants suit that distorted her slender curves, and her hand raised as if by helium and clutched her jacket closed in woman's universal reaction to distress.

"This is Alo Nudger, Joan," Alison said gently.

Joan stared at me, without surprise now. She looked worse than her photograph. The upturned nose lent her a wary, haunted expression that matched the hollowness of her eyes. Her hair was much lighter than in her snapshots, cut short and carelessly tousled.

"Alison's told me about you," she said in a calm voice. She was about to say something else, then caught herself and stared at me with cautious appraisal.

"You don't have to worry now about Congram or Gratuity Insirance," I said.

Something flared in her eyes for a second, something I couldn't decipher. "You know about them?"

"Just enough," I said. "I'd like for you to tell me the rest. It's the only way now, the best way."

She seemed to withdraw to someplace beyond me to consider that, walking absently to a chocolate-colored sofa and sitting lightly.

"You're working for my father," she said, as if it were an accusation.

"And for you, Joan. At this point your interests are the same."

Alison sat next to her, rested a soft hand on her arm. "He's right, Joan. You should see your only way out of it now. Do what he asks."

Joan laughed, almost a bitter sort of cough, and looked up at me. "You're not going to tell me my father's concerned with my safety?"

I shook my head. "I'm not going to pass judgment on your father. All I said was that your interests coincide."

"I don't have to go back."

"No, and if you do go, you don't have to stay."

Joan leaned back on the sofa, breathed out her uncertainty and tension in a long sigh. She'd reached a decision; for everybody's sake, I hoped the right one.

"All right," she said, "what do you want me to do?"

I sat opposite her in an armless chair. "From the beginning, tell me about Victor Talbert and Gratuity Insurance."

She didn't move; her dark eyes locked on something low and invisible on the other side of the room. "I loved Vic. . . . We loved each other. And things were beautiful until he lost his job." Now she did look at me, frowning and haggard despite her youth. "You have to understand what losing the job meant to Vic, what a crushing thing it was to him. He was ambitious, hard working and dedicated—not just to his job but to everything he did. The idea that he might fail never entered his mind, because he wouldn't let it. Nobody wanted success more, or feared failure as much."

I waited for her to continue and didn't say I could have introduced her to more than a few Victor Talberts.

"Vic tried to get another job," Joan continued, "and he could have had several with starting salaries and responsibilities below what he considered his level. He refused them, out of personal and professioanl pride. Then he decided to go into business for himself, and he went all over trying to get financing, but no one would give him a loan. That's when he began to get sour on himself, really depressed, and that's when Jerry Congram came along."

"Had he known Talbert before?"

"No, Congram said his 'research and recruiting department' had recommended Vic to him. Vic was impressed with Jerry. So was I and so was everybody. Jerry can tell you things, make you believe in yourself, make you believe almost anything. When he was gone, sometimes you'd begin to wonder. . . . But then he'd be back, with all his fire and all his belief. I'll admit, Vic and I were dazzled, and Vic had hope again, and something to suit his abilities."

"A position with Gratuity Insurance?"

Joan nodded her head, kept it bowed.

"Joan, I need to know how Gratuity Insurance works, how many people are involved."

She didn't hesitate. "There were fifteen, including Vic. I wasn't actually an employee, but I was going to be and Congram trusted me. Congram recruited junior executives and other strongly business-oriented people to work for him. He was very careful; he'd learn everything about someone before even considering approaching them for recruitment. Everyone has to be loyal to him, ambitious, aggressive, and believe in the system."

"What system?"

She looked at me curiously and moved an arm in an encompassing wave. "Why, everything . . . the way things work. Only without the hindrance of self-doubt. Jerry believes in realism without rationalization, self-honesty and the decisiveness to act on fact and not fancy. . . ." She seemed to realize that she was parroting someone else's words and thoughts, and her voice faded. Her jaw muscles flexed and she swallowed before continuing.

"Every Gratuity employee is extensively trained," she said, "before actually being used in the field. A trained agent will gain audience with a carefully chosen top executive on whatever pretense will work best. Then, in private, the agent implies that one of the few in the business hierarchy above the chosen executive has sent him, and if Gratuity's instructions are followed, certain obstacles to advancement will be removed."

She was parroting again, but telling me what I wanted to know.

"If the executive doesn't follow Gratuity's instructions, he'll suffer the consequences. Sometimes that would be an arranged accident, or even a false suicide complete with a note the victim was forced to sign. The agent instructs the executive to bring about some minor policy changes that will in some obscure way benefit one or more of his superiors. All this is used for is a convincer. Then the executive is assured that what is happening to him is now common practice, and surely he must understand, as did his superiors, that if he goes to the police or in any way fails to comply, not only will he destroy his career, but he must be killed as a matter of minimizing projected risk factors. The names of other Gratuity subjects like himself are mentioned to him and he's warned not to contact them. These are names of subjects who are classified as risks. When some of these names appear in the obituary columns, it serves as the clincher on the deal. At that point the executive is instructed to send large sums of company money to an anonymous address, which is how Gratuity Insurance derives its income. When a predetermined sum, which only Jerry knows, is reached, the company will be liquidated."

"It boils down to simple extortion," I said.

Joan's eyes were vague and dark, somehow innocent. "It's simply business, Mr. Nudger, business without hypocrisy." She seemed to realize what she'd said and looked away. But there was nothing to look at but extortion and murder, and her own fear.

"How many 'projected risk factors' were actually killed?" I asked.

"I don't know. . . . A small percentage, according

to Jerry. After the initial contact, the subject is watched closely for a while. Sometimes, if he does anything suspicious, Gratuity breaks off all contact with him rather than eliminate him and use him as an example. And if a subject goes to the police, he won't be killed. Too much danger to the operation."

"The operation, the company, was everything, wasn't it?"

"It was more important than any one of us," Joan said with fervor, despite the past tense. "Jerry held meetings as often as possible, and each meeting began with a short oath of allegiance to the company. There was no way not to be caught up in the zealousness and the feeling of purpose."

"What made Victor Talbert want out?"

"Jerry was away for more than a week, long enough for his personality and his ideas to lose some of their effect on us. And Vic got his loan. It was too late then— Jerry would never let him go. But Vic knew he could have made it without Congram and Gratuity, and that seemed to change him. We decided to run."

"From the apartment on Oakner?"

She seemed surprised as she nodded, raking her fingers through her mussed hair in an oddly careless gesture.

"Why did you choose Layton, feeling as you do about your father?"

"Vic and I knew what would happen if Gratuity found us. We thought that by giving the impression we were under my father's protection, even if we really weren't, it might stop them or at least give us time. So we moved to a little house in Layton, calling ourselves David and Joan Branly, and kept it a secret from everyone."

"How did you sell that idea to Melissa?"

"We let her continue to call herself Melissa Clark, and we told some of the neighbors I was divorced and she'd kept her father's name."

"But Congram found you," I said.

"Yes, and he tried to talk us into rejoining Gratuity. Jerry promised Vic everything—money, position. . . . He was convincing. But Vic refused and I chose to stay with him. We swore to Jerry we'd keep our former affiliation with Gratuity a secret, and he pretended to believe us on the basis that we'd be incriminating ourselves if we talked. But he showed us a newspaper with a story about a Gratuity-arranged death, and he had the back of the house sprayed with bullets that night to demonstrate how easily he could deal with us if we did talk. I think he really did all that just to convince us that he thought we were scared enough to remain silent, and to make us think he was sincere about leaving us alone. But all he was doing was trying to figure out the best way to get rid of us without suspicion. Vic and I didn't believe him, and we decided to move again. Then Vic. . . ."

"I know," I said, thinking of the photos of the young man in the blood-spattered jacket.

Joan clenched her fists hard enough to whiten the flesh. "I didn't know what to do. . . . I was terrified, for myself and for Melissa. I packed what I could. I didn't dare take Melissa; I was afraid she might be killed along with me. So I left her with the next-door neighbor and took a bus to Orlando."

Probably that was what Congram wanted, I thought, to get her away from Layton to where she could be killed without an intensive investigation, just another unidentifiable corpse in the bowels of some large city.

"I didn't know what to do," Joan said, "where to go. I left Orlando. Then I stayed in New Orleans for a while, but I never felt safe, and I was running out of money and hope. Finally I thought of Alison, the things she'd done for me, how she'd told me to come to her if I ever needed help. And I remembered what she did for a living."

And wound up here with very little hope, I thought. I

felt sorrow for Joan Clark, for whom a lot of things had ended, if not her life.

"You have to understand, Mr. Nudger, Gratuity employees don't see themselves as criminals. We—they are ambitious and aggressive business people, in a close-knit enterprise, who simply are carrying the precepts of business to ultimate reaches, where they're headed anyway." The autonomous voice had taken over again, the rote excuses for exploitation and murder. "Visionaries ahead of their time," she added, "no more criminals than the manufacturers of unsafe but profitable products that endanger life, no more extortionists than the lobbyists who twist the appropriate arms with personal knowledge to gain favorable treatment. Vic wasn't evil. He became what Congram told him he was—a genuinely honest businessman, a pragmatist without rationalization or apology."

"Do you believe that, Joan?"

Her body was trembling. "I did . . . and some of it I still do."

I understood her lingering belief. Gratuity's success depended upon its victims' believing that someone above them in their organization would employ polished potential killers in the course of business. And with relatively few exceptions, like Manners and Blount, the victims believed—and paid.

I couldn't blame them. I'd have paid. Manners and Blount and Tad Osborne should have paid.

"Melissa is with Gordon," I told Joan.

"I know. Alison found out for me. I was afraid to try to see her."

"You'll see her shortly," I said. "Then I'd like you to see your father."

"Is it safe? Is it over?"

"Almost. The dangerous part."

I could see that something in her mind rejected what I'd said while every other part of her wanted to accept

178

it. Her thin body squirmed on the sofa, and she began to cry away the part that rejected.

Alison hugged her, appeared close to crying herself. Wouldn't that have been something to see? I got up, paced, and casually brushed the moisture that threatened my own right eye.

I used Alison's phone to call Dale Carlon. After explaining the situation to him and accepting his thanks, I let him talk to Joan.

Whatever his reasons, Carlon must have expressed heartfelt relief to Joan at finding her safe, because by the time she'd hung up the phone I could tell that things were at least bearable between father and daughter.

"What now?" Alison asked.

"Now you stay here with Joan," I said. "For the time being, this is still the safest place for her."

"Where are you going?"

"Where you wanted me to go in the first place. The police."

I told Joan and Alison that I'd be back and left the apartment, thinking of my soon-to-be fifty-thousand-dollar bank account. The drop in the elevator was somehow soothing, like a dropping away from my problems.

It's that way sometimes after you've punched the down button.

25

I got directions to the nearest precinct station, an old brownstone building with arched and shadeless windows.

The inside of the building was similar to that of a thousand other precinct houses, caged booking counter, interrogation cubicles, several steel-gray desks supporting typewriters, wire baskets and telephones. From a receiver somewhere, the ever-present crackling voices of a dispatcher and the answering cars read like a litany. Familiarity with this scene was a part of me.

At the desk a sergeant was talking to a plainclothesman. I walked over and identified myself as a private investigator, bringing about momentary interest, then polite boredom.

As I told my story, I could see that Sergeant Hartenstein was my main obstacle. He refused to believe that any matter was urgent or actionable without predetermination of every insignificant fact. He was a ruddy-faced, gray-haired man with a perfectly trimmed mustache, a slow and correct thinker. I was reminded of Sergeant Avery, in Layton.

"You say they're an insurance company?" Hartenstein asked, rolling a broken-clipped ball-point between sausage fingers.

"They say that," I told him.

His blue eyes shifted to the right and looked past me at a tall, broad-shouldered man in a lieutenant's uniform. The man had straight black hair, watery, sensitive dark eyes and an oversized nose that hadn't been set after a break.

Sergeant Hartenstein looked relieved, his facial muscles noticeably relaxing. "Tell your story to Lieutenant Morri," he said.

I did.

"That's beyond our jurisdiction," the lieutenant said, looking inscrutable and scratching the side of his neck.

"I figured that. Don't you have a cooperative arrangement with these other departments?"

"Sure, under certain circumstances, or if they request it."

"Who's your superior?" I asked him.

The lieutenant didn't care for the question, but he gave me the name and phone number of a captain.

I asked if I could use the phone, and they pointed to a black wall phone near the interrogation cubicles. On the gray-painted wall around the phone were penciled dozens of phone numbers, most of which probably belonged to bondsmen or lawyers.

Lieutenant Morri seemed worried, but he didn't have to be. Instead of phoning the captain, I called Dale Carlon.

The situation enraged Carlon. He said he wasn't sure what he could do, but that he'd do something. Money speaks louder than words and usually has the final say. But we were a long way from Layton. When I hung up, I mentally gave Carlon a slightly better than even chance of being able to make things happen.

One thing Carlon definitely hadn't made happen was the arrival of the press. But nobody's flawless. The press was with us at Devon Acres, equipped with cameras, recorders and mobile TV unit vans.

Lights still glowed in the windows of the house of the Gratuity meeting, as they did in the windows of the other completed houses scattered about the graded development. The night seemed darker, and I tried to stay out of the way while the operation took form.

I remembered when, years ago, my brother had sold life insurance and I'd helped him work on his sales approach. The company he sold for had used, on tough customers, a tactic they called "the hard sell death knell." "If tomorrow you die . . ." was the salesman's opening line of the horror story. Gratuity Insurance had assumed control of the "if" of that opening line.

Within minutes, exits from Devon Acres were blocked, and men were stationed in the wooded area to cut off a retreat in that direction.

Several unmarked cars drove up slowly to park around the house, then four patrol cars rushed to block the driveway and park in strategic positions along the street. I saw several dark shadows move swiftly to the rear of the house. Car doors swung open, figures crouched, and I saw the thick barrels of riot guns. Police from three departments were ready for a shootout if necessary.

Cued by a radio command, dozens of spotlights popped into brilliance and were trained on the sprawling ranch house, giving it the unnaturally bright, unshadowed look of a movie set.

The law had provided the lights, the press the cameras. Whether or not there would be action depended on Jerry Congram.

The major who was in command asked, in a polite but professionally firm voice, for the occupants of the house to come out unarmed. He then explained to them that they had no choice. But for the lights that shone in the windows and the cars lining the driveway, he might have been talking to an empty house. Beside me a man braced on a patrol car fender kept a portable TV camera aimed at the spotlighted house while he murmured something I couldn't understand under his breath.

The major with the bullhorn repeated his instructions.

Around me there was talk of tear gas, of high-density firepower.

Then the front door opened, and Congram led them out.

There were ten of them—six men and four women—all walking with hands raised to shoulder height, squinting at the brightness concentrated on them. Some of them appeared frightened, some baffled. Congram looked like a man whose worst suspicions had been confirmed. His expression was resigned, enduring, distantly amused.

As the line of Gratuity employees reached the police, there were flurries of motion and the clamping on of handcuffs. Several armed patrolmen rushed into the house through the front door, seeking more prisoners. Everyone around me began to close in on the now-diffuse scene.

The press sensed right away that Congram was the leader; he had that about him. He was leaning against the door of a police car, his wrists handcuffed behind him. I heard him patiently, even condescendingly, explaining to a reporter that a man is guilty only if established as such in a court of law.

"You maintain your innocence?" the reporter asked.

Congram addressed his answer to the half-dozen microphones thrust at him. "Of course. I'm as innocent as any of you. The only *wrongdoing* one can commit is the mistake that leads to his conviction and labels what actions he's taken as unethical or immoral. Until that conviction, no *wrong* act has really been committed. In the truest sense, the crime is in being caught. You all know that."

They acted as if they agreed with him.

"Innocent until proved guilty is the basis of our society . . ." he began, but his lecture was interrupted by the arrival of the police van to transport the Gratuity employees to holdover cells. They cooperated with the police in brisk, businesslike fashion so that the van was loaded in less than a minute. Congram was the last inside, and he nodded pleasantly to the officer holding the door open and climbed into the van without hesitation. One of the reporters yelled something about another Manson cult, but Congram ignored him, sat down and seemed to order the officer to close the van doors.

In a way I had to admire Congram, which was what made him dangerous. He was the ultimate and inevitable extension of the system itself and, though he would deny it, the product of compromise.

One after another, engines roared to life around me, as if at the beginning of a race. I started walking to where my own car was parked. It was time to return to Alison's apartment.

"How do you figure in this?" someone asked me.

I pretended not to have heard the question and walked on, unsure of the answer.

26

The day after Gratuity's unexpected "liquidation" Carlon arrived in Chicago with a battery of anonymous-looking lawyers. I talked to some of them, filling them in on what the police might have missed telling them, and found them to be sharp, cold individuals. They pondered legal angles that sounded ridiculous until they discussed them so seriously that they became serious.

During the course of the day, I managed to break through to Carlon once, for a brief and interrupted phone conversation. His lawyers accounted for his inaccessibility with explanations that sounded reasonable when said fast.

Carlon did manage to have his daughter free within hours. Whether Joan Clark was out on bond or hadn't had charges brought against her I didn't know and didn't think to ask her when she phoned to thank me. I accepted her thanks with a humility befitting one of the finest investigators in the country, not mentioning the exorbitant fee her father had agreed to pay me for risking my life.

For a while, the police gave me a hard time about withholding evidence, but some old connections I had put in some words for me. Carlon also interceded, though in this instance he couldn't be of much help. It could have turned out worse. I escaped prosecution and was sure I'd be able to retain my investigator's license, but I'd never operate again in Chicago. I could stand that. Before Joan hung up I asked her to tell her father I was on my way over to thank him personally for his efforts on my behalf.

When I got there, Carlon was out.

It was past noon the next day before he deigned to see me in his suite at the Continental Plaza. I didn't know whether to be angry about his inaccessibility or grateful to him for helping to get the police off me.

When I walked into Carlon's opulent suite, he shook my hand enthusiastically and bared his teeth in his PR smile, making me more confused. One thing I wasn't confused about was the remaining forty thousand dollars he owed me.

Carlon was wearing leather slippers and some sort of patterned blue silk lounging robe. He sat down slowly in an overstuffed chair in the manner of a king situating himself on a throne. "I can't thank you enough, Nudger," he said earnestly, "and neither can Joan."

"Fifty thousand dollars is more than adequate thanks," I said. I found myself ill at ease in the luxurious suite, with my wrinkled bargain suit and the scratches from the Devon Acres woods still marking my hands and face.

"Actually I've been trying to contact you to talk about that for the past few days," Carlon said, and I felt a chill of suspicion dance up my spine, catch in my throat as a lump.

I wanted to speak, didn't know if I could manage it or what I should say.

"I've had my accountant draw up a check for you," Carlon said and held out a pale-blue and beautiful rectangle of paper.

Letting out my breath, I leaned forward and accepted it from him.

When I looked at the check, I saw that it was for five thousand dollars, and I felt a weight settle in my stomach. I was afraid of the rage that was pulsing through me. My voice was strained and distant. "You're thirty-five thousand short. . . ."

Somehow Carlon managed to look surprised. There wasn't a hint of insincerity in his handsome face or concerned gray eyes. "Of course you realized the remainder of the fee was predicated upon certain circumstances in Joan's disappearance."

"It was predicated upon my finding her," I said tightly. Behind Carlon his male secretary had entered the room and begun to busy himself about a cluttered desk.

"Let me point out," Carlon said, "that the investigation has revealed nothing criminal, nothing legally actionable, in Joan's involvement. My lawyers and the police have questioned her extensively. She was never actually a part of that establishment Manson cult."

"That seems to me to be beside the point."

He appeared puzzled. "It was Joan's welfare that this was all about, wasn't it?"

"That and fifty thousand dollars." I was getting angrier now, feeling the loss I knew I couldn't avoid.

"That seems a rather mercenary point of view," Carlon said. Then his voice became tolerant. "You must

186

see this for what it was—a business arrangement. There is, after all, not even any written record of our agreement—"

"Our agreement was about fifty thousand dollars," I interrupted, "and I was to collect it when I located your daughter."

He shook his head as if losing patience with a backward child. "Believe me, Mr. Nudger, the conversation wasn't exactly as you remember it. The full remainder of the fee was predicated upon certain conditions. Why, any impartial judge—"

"I know I can't sue you. There's nothing in writing. And since you've somehow managed to get Joan off the hook legally, I can't endanger her case in court."

"You seem to grasp those essentials," Carlon said. "Why can't you grasp the fact that you were involved in a very profitable business deal, though not so wildly profitable as your imagination had led you to believe? I wish you could recall the exact details of our conversation in Layton." He seemed to believe it. I don't think any polygraph would have tripped him up. "The five thousand dollars," he said, nodding toward the check in my hand, "is as much a gesture of appreciation as anything."

I knew what he meant. He could still stop payment on what he'd given me, which would be a considerable amount of money even after I'd paid my expenses. The weight in my stomach seemed to expand, driving the anger from me and replacing it with resignation. I was disgusted with myself for feeling even a vague gratitude toward Carlon for what he had paid me. Though legally he owed me nothing.

The desire to get really nasty with him, even violent, left me then. I did have ten thousand dollars in the bank. And any outburst would cost me five thousand, in itself more than I'd ever been paid for a single case.

I'd be damned, though, if I'd thank Carlon for his

"gesture of appreciation." Stuffing the check into my shirt pocket, I left him without saying anything.

Some small satisfaction.

It was winter and I was home in my house trailer, lounging on the sofa, watching the six o'clock news, when next I saw Dale Carlon. He was standing before richly flowered wallpaper somewhere, pleasantly and patiently explaining to a network newsman how a rise in plastics prices now would actually save the consumer money in the future. Gee, he was convincing!

Later that evening I thought I'd catch the Carlton interview again on the ten o'clock news. But during the weather forecast, the picture on my portable TV suddenly shrank to a tiny, brilliant square of light, revolved and disappeared.

I went to the metal box where I kept my important papers and dug out the set's warranty.

It had expired the week before.

CARROLL & GRAF

FINE MYSTERY AND SUSPENSE
TITLES FROM CARROLL & GRAF

- ☐ Allingham, Margery/MR. CAMPION'S FARTHING — $3.95
- ☐ Allingham, Margery/MR. CAMPION'S QUARRY — $3.95
- ☐ Allingham, Margery/NO LOVE LOST — $3.95
- ☐ Allingham, Margery/THE WHITE COTTAGE MYSTERY — $3.50
- ☐ Ambler, Eric/BACKGROUND TO DANGER — $3.95
- ☐ Ambler, Eric/CAUSE FOR ALARM — $3.95
- ☐ Ambler, Eric/A COFFIN FOR DIMITRIOS — $3.95
- ☐ Ambler, Eric/EPITAPH FOR A SPY — $3.95
- ☐ Ambler, Eric/STATE OF SIEGE — $3.95
- ☐ Ambler, Eric/JOURNEY INTO FEAR — $3.95
- ☐ Ball, John/THE KIWI TARGET — $3.95
- ☐ Bentley, E.C./TRENT'S OWN CASE — $3.95
- ☐ Blake, Nicholas/A TANGLED WEB — $3.50
- ☐ Brand, Christianna/DEATH IN HIGH HEELS — $3.95
- ☐ Brand, Christianna/GREEN FOR DANGER — $3.95
- ☐ Brand, Christianna/FOG OF DOUBT — $3.50
- ☐ Brand, Christianna/TOUR DE FORCE — $3.95
- ☐ Brown, Fredric/THE LENIENT BEAST — $3.50
- ☐ Brown, Fredric/MURDER CAN BE FUN — $3.95
- ☐ Brown, Fredric/THE SCREAMING MIMI — $3.50
- ☐ Browne, Howard/THIN AIR — $3.50
- ☐ Buchan, John/JOHN MACNAB — $3.95
- ☐ Buchan, John/WITCH WOOD — $3.95
- ☐ Burnett, W.R./LITTLE CAESAR — $3.50
- ☐ Butler, Gerald/KISS THE BLOOD OFF MY HANDS — $3.95
- ☐ Carr, John Dickson/CAPTAIN CUT-THROAT — $3.95
- ☐ Carr, John Dickson/DARK OF THE MOON — $3.50
- ☐ Carr, John Dickson/THE DEMONIACS — $3.95
- ☐ Carr, John Dickson/FIRE, BURN! — $3.50
- ☐ Carr, John Dickson/THE GHOSTS' HIGH NOON — $3.95

- [ ] Carr, John Dickson/NINE WRONG ANSWERS $3.50
- [ ] Carr, John Dickson/PAPA LA-BAS $3.95
- [ ] Carr, John Dickson/THE WITCH OF THE LOW TIDE $3.95
- [ ] Chesterton, G. K./THE MAN WHO KNEW TOO MUCH $3.95
- [ ] Chesterton, G. K./THE MAN WHO WAS THURSDAY $3.50
- [ ] Coles, Manning/ALL THAT GLITTERS $3.95
- [ ] Coles, Manning/THE FIFTH MAN $2.95
- [ ] Coles, Manning/THE MAN IN THE GREEN HAT $3.50
- [ ] Coles, Manning/NO ENTRY $3.50
- [ ] Collins, Michael/WALK A BLACK WIND $3.95
- [ ] Crofts, Freeman Wills/THE CASK $3.95
- [ ] Crofts, Freeman Wills/INSPECTOR FRENCH'S GREATEST CASE $3.50
- [ ] Dewey, Thomas B./THE MEAN STREETS $3.50
- [ ] Dickson, Carter/THE CURSE OF THE BRONZE LAMP $3.50
- [ ] Disch, Thomas M & Sladek, John/BLACK ALICE $3.95
- [ ] Eberhart, Mignon/MESSAGE FROM HONG KONG $3.50
- [ ] Eastlake, William/CASTLE KEEP $3.50
- [ ] Farrell, Henry/WHAT EVER HAPPENED TO BABY JANE? $3.95
- [ ] Fennelly, Tony/THE CLOSET HANGING $3.50
- [ ] Freeling, Nicolas/LOVE IN AMSTERDAM $3.95
- [ ] Freeman, R. Austin/THE EYE OF OSIRIS $3.95
- [ ] Freeman, R. Austin/MYSTERY OF ANGELINA FROOD $3.95
- [ ] Freeman, R. Austin/THE RED THUMB MARK $3.50
- [ ] Gardner, Erle Stanley/DEAD MEN'S LETTERS $4.50
- [ ] Gilbert, Michael/ANYTHING FOR A QUIET LIFE $3.95
- [ ] Gilbert, Michael/THE DOORS OPEN $3.95
- [ ] Gilbert, Michael/THE 92nd TIGER $3.95
- [ ] Gilbert, Michael/OVERDRIVE $3.95

☐ Waugh, Hillary/A DEATH IN A TOWN $3.95
☐ Waugh, Hillary/LAST SEEN WEARING $3.95
☐ Waugh, Hillary/SLEEP LONG, MY LOVE $3.95
☐ Westlake, Donald E./THE MERCENARIES $3.95
☐ Willeford, Charles/THE WOMAN CHASER $3.95
☐ Wilson, Colin/A CRIMINAL HISTORY OF
   MANKIND $13.95

Available from fine bookstores everywhere or use this coupon for ordering.